SAVING MADDIE'S BABY

BY
MARION LENNOX

MILLS & BOON

® and TM are trademarks owned and used by the trademark owner
and/or its licensee. Trademarks marked with ® are registered with the
United Kingdom Patent Office and/or the Office for Harmonisation in
the Internal Market and in other countries.

Published in Great Britain 2016
By Mills & Boon, an imprint of HarperCollins*Publishers*
1 London Bridge Street, London, SE1 9GF

© 2016 Marion Lennox

ISBN: 978-0-263-26386-2

Our policy is to use papers that are natural, renewable and recyclable
products and made from wood grown in sustainable forests. The logging
and manufacturing processes conform to the legal environmental
regulations of the country of origin.

Printed and bound in Great Britain
by CPI Antony Rowe, Chippenham, Wiltshire

Marion Lennox has written over a hundred romance novels and is published in over a hundred countries and thirty languages. Her international awards include the prestigious RITA® Award (twice) and the *RT Book Reviews* Career Achievement award for 'a body of work which makes us laugh and teaches us about love'. Marion adores her family, her kayak, her dog, and lying on the beach with a book someone else has written. Heaven.

Books by Marion Lennox

Mills & Boon Medical Romance

The Surgeon's Doorstep Baby
Miracle on Kaimotu Island
Gold Coast Angels: A Doctor's Redemption
Waves of Temptation
A Secret Shared...
Meant-to-Be Family
From Christmas to Forever?

Mills & Boon Cherish

A Bride for the Maverick Millionaire
Sparks Fly with the Billionaire
Christmas at the Castle
Nine Months to Change His Life
Christmas Where They Belong

Visit the Author Profile page
at millsandboon.co.uk for more titles.

To Meredith and Alison,
who make my writer's life fun.

PROLOGUE

HEROES AND HEROINES don't choose to be brave, Maddie decided. Mostly they have bravery thrust upon them. In her particular case, a heroine was created when vast chunks of rock trapped one doctor in an underground mine, a mine she should never have been near in the first place.

This heroine wasn't brave. This heroine was stupid.

Everyone knew the mine was dangerous. Ian Lockhart, the owner, had left Wildfire Island weeks ago, with salaries unpaid and debts outstanding. The mine had been closed for non-compliance with safety standards not long after Ian's disappearance.

So whose bright idea had it been to see if they could tap one of the seams close to the surface?

There were reasons this seam hadn't been tapped before. The rock was brittle. Without salaries, though, and desperate for income, the islanders had cut through the fence and quietly burrowed. No one was supposed to know.

But now… The call had come through an hour ago. A splintered piece of shoring timber and a minor rockfall had left one of the islanders with a fractured leg.

If it hadn't been badly fractured they might have brought Kalifa down to the hospital, keeping their mining secret. Instead, his mates had had the sense to ring

Maddie, asking her to come across the mountains to the overgrown mine site.

Maddie—Madeline Haddon—was heavily pregnant but she was the only doctor available. The miners had told her there were shards of bone puncturing Kalifa's skin, so transporting him by road before assessment meant the risk of cutting off the blood supply.

She'd had to go.

Once at the mine site, it had taken work to stabilise him. Kalifa needed specialist surgery if he wasn't to be left with a permanent limp, and she was worried about the strain on his heart. She'd just rung Keanu, the other island doctor, who was currently on his way back from a clinic on an outer island. She'd been asking him to organise Kalifa's evacuation to Cairns when there was an ominous rumble from underground.

The mouth of the mine had belched a vast cloud of dirt and dust.

She'd thought Kalifa and the two friends who'd called her had been working alone. She'd never imagined there were men still in there. Surely not? But out they came, staggering, blinded by dust.

She'd been helping lift Kalifa into the back of the jeep—her jeep was set up as a no-frills ambulance, used in emergencies for patient transport. She'd turned and gazed in horror as the miners stumbled out.

'How many of you are down there?' The guy out first had a jagged gash on his arm. She grabbed a dressing and applied pressure.

'Tw-twelve,' the guy told her.

'Are you all out now?' When they'd rung about Kalifa she'd assumed... Why hadn't she asked?

'Three still to come.'

'Why? Where are they?'

'Malu's smashed his leg,' the guy told her. 'He's bleeding like a stuck pig.'

'Is he stuck? Has the shaft caved right in?'

'Just…just a bit of a rockfall where Kalifa fell against the shoring timber. Malu got unlucky—we were trying to shore it up again and he was right underneath where it fell. Macca and Reuben are helping him out but they had to stop to tighten the tourniquet. But the shaft's clear enough in front of the fall. They'll be out soon.' His voice faltered. 'As long as they can stop the bleeding.'

She stared at the mine mouth in dismay.

The dust was settling. It was looking almost normal.

Bleeding out…

Oh, help.

She'd done a swift, sweeping assessment of those around her. No one seemed in immediate distress. Men were already helping each other. The nurse who'd accompanied her, Caroline Lockhart, was taking care of a miner who looked like he'd fractured his arm. He was still standing, not in obvious danger. A couple of the men were crouched on the ground, coughing. They should be checked.

Triage.

One broken arm. Bruises, lacerations, nothing else obvious. Kalifa was waiting to be transferred to hospital.

Bleeding out…

Triage told her exactly where she was needed.

But she was pregnant. Pregnant! Instinctively her hand went to her belly, cringing at what she was contemplating.

What was the risk?

This had been a minor rockfall, she'd told herself. The shaft was still clear.

Along that shaft, Malu was bleeding to death. She had no choice.

'Help me,' she snapped at an uninjured miner. She

grabbed his hand, pressing it onto the pad she'd made on his mate's bleeding arm. 'Push hard and keep up the pressure until Caroline has time to help you. The bleeding's already easing but don't let go. Caroline, can you radio Keanu?'

'He's on his way in from Atangi.'

'Tell him to land the boat on this side of the island and get here as fast as he can. Meanwhile, don't move Kalifa. He needs a doctor with him during transfer. The blood supply to the leg's stable, as long as he doesn't shift. But he has enough pain relief on board to keep him comfortable. Meanwhile, give me your torch,' she snapped at another miner. 'And your hard hat.'

'Y-you can't go in there,' the miner stammered. 'Doc, you're pregnant. It's dangerous.'

'Of course it's dangerous. You've been working in a mine that's supposed to be closed, you morons. But what choice do I have? Malu's got two children and his wife's my friend. Caro, you're in charge.'

And she picked up her bag, shoved on a hard hat and headed into the shaft.

'Doc, wait, I'll come with you,' one of the miners yelled after her.

'Don't even think about it. You have children, too,' she snapped back. 'We now have four idiots in the mine. Don't anyone dare make it five.'

CHAPTER ONE

DR JOSHUA CAMPBELL was so bored with solitaire he'd resorted to cheating to finish each game faster. It defeated the purpose, but he'd read every journal he could get his hands on. He'd checked and rechecked equipment. He'd paced. He was driving the rest of the staff at Cairns Air Sea Rescue Service nuts. He was going out of his mind.

No one in Northern Queensland seemed to have done so much as stand on a spider for the whole week. He'd been rostered for patient transfers, and every one of them had been routine. Patients had either been heading home, or were being flown from the city hospital to the country hospitals where they could continue recuperation among friends. There'd not been a single emergency amongst them.

'If this keeps up I'm joining the army,' Josh grumbled to Beth, his paramedic colleague. 'Maybe there's a place for me in the bomb squad. Do you suppose there's any call for bomb disposal any place around here?'

'You could try cleaning our kitchen as practice,' Beth said morosely. 'School holidays and three teenage boys? I'd defy a hand grenade to make more mess. You need to try a touch of domesticity if you want explosions. Consider marriage.'

'Been there, got the T-shirt,' he muttered.

'That's right, with Maddie, but that's ancient history.'
Beth and Josh had joined the service at the same time,
and after years of working together there was little they
didn't know about each other. 'You hardly stuck around
long enough to feel the full force of domestic bliss.' And
then her smile faded. 'Whoops, sorry, Josh, I know you
lost the baby, but still… It was so long ago. You and Karen,
you think you might…?'

'No!' He said it with more vehemence than he'd meant
to use. In fact, he startled himself. They were in the staff
office, in the corner of the great hangar that held the service planes. The door was open and Josh's vehemence
echoed out into the vaulted hangar. 'No,' he repeated, more
mildly. 'Domesticity doesn't interest either of us.'

'And you're seeing less of each other,' Beth said thought-
fully. 'Moving on? Seeing we're quiet, you want to check
some dating sites? We might just find *the one*.'

'Beth…'

'You're thirty-six years old, Josh. Okay, you still have
the looks. Indeed you do. It drives me nuts, seeing the way
old ladies melt when you smile. But your looks'll fade, my
lad. You'll be on your walker before you know it, gumming
your crusts, bewailing not having a grandchild to dandle…'

'I'm definitely applying for the bomb squad,' he retorted, and tossed a sheaf of paper at her. 'Just to get away
from you. Sort these for a change. They're already sorted
but so what? Give me some peace so I can download a
bomb squad application.'

And then the radio buzzed into life. They both made a
grab, but Beth got there first. She listened to the curt instructions on the other end and her face set.

The tossed papers lay ignored on the floor. Josh was already reaching for his jacket. He knew that look. 'What?'
he demanded as she finished.

'Trouble,' Beth said, snagging her jacket, as well. 'Mine collapse on Wildfire Island. One smashed leg, needs evac to the orthopods in Cairns. Plane's leaving in ten.'

'Mine collapse?' He was snapping queries as he got organised. 'Just the one injury?'

'He was injured at the start of it. One of the supports collapsed. Fell on this guy's leg but the rest of the idiots didn't see it as a sign they should evacuate. But now...' She took a deep breath. 'The collapse looks serious. We're working on early information but one of the local doctors is trapped, as well.'

One of the local doctors.

Wildfire.

And something inside seemed to freeze.

Beth stopped, too. 'Josh? What is it?'

'You said Wildfire. Part of the M'Langi group?'

'Yeah.'

'That's where Maddie's working.'

'Maddie?' Her eyes widened as she understood. 'Your Maddie?'

'We're not married.' It was a dumb thing to say but it was all he could think of.

'I know that. You haven't been married for years. So how do you know she's there?'

'I sort of...keep tabs. She's working fly in, fly out, two weeks there, one week on the mainland. Her mum's still in a nursing home in Cairns.'

'Right.' Beth started gathering gear again and he moved into automatic mode and did the same. There was a moment's loaded silence, and then...

'You mean you stalk her?' she demanded, but he knew it was Beth's way of making things light. Making a joke...

'I do not stalk!'

'But you keep tabs.' There was little to add to their bags,

only the drugs they kept locked away or refrigerated. 'It sounds creepy.'

'We keep in touch. Sort of. Christmas and birthdays. And I take note of where she's registered to work. In case...' He hesitated. 'Hell, I don't know. In case of nothing.'

Beth's face softened. She clipped her bag closed, then touched his shoulder as she straightened. 'I know,' she said. 'I've been married twice, remember. Once your ex, always your ex. Unless it's nasty there's always a little bit of them under your skin. But, hey, there's a sizeable med centre on Wildfire. The trapped doctor doesn't have to be Maddie.'

'Right.' But suddenly he was staring into middle distance. He knew... Somehow he knew.

'Earth to Josh,' Beth said, not so gently now. 'The plane's waiting. Let's go.'

The crash had come from nowhere. One minute Maddie was working efficiently in the dim light, worried but not terrified.

Now she was terrified.

She needed to block out the dust and dark and fear.

Where was her patient?

She'd lost her torch. She'd fallen, stumbling in terror as the rock wall had crashed around her. She was okay, she decided, pushing her way cautiously to her knees. There was still breathable air if she covered her mouth and breathed through a slit in her fingers. But she couldn't see.

Somewhere in here was a guy with a life-threatening bleed.

Where was the torch?

Phone app. She practically sobbed with relief as she remembered an afternoon a few weeks ago, sitting on the hospital terrace with Wildfire's charge nurse, Hettie, while

Caroline had shown them apps they could put on their cell phones.

Most she had no use for, but the torch app had looked useful for things such as checking it was a gecko on her nose and not a spider in the middle of the night. The disadvantages of living in the tropics. But now... Yes! Her phone was in her jacket pocket. She grabbed it and flicked it on.

One push and a surprising amount of light fought through the dust.

She could now see the big torch, lying at her feet. She grabbed it. The switch had flicked off when it had fallen. Not broken. She had light.

Next...

The guy she'd come in for.

She'd met them halfway in. Blood had been streaming from Malu's thigh and he'd been barely conscious. The miners with him had tied a tourniquet but it wasn't enough.

'He needs more pressure,' she'd snapped. 'Put him down.'

And then she'd felt the rumbles. She'd felt the earth tremble.

'Run!' she'd screamed at the two guys who'd been carrying him, and she still seemed to hear the echoes of that yell.

They'd run.

She hoped they'd made it. Fallen rock was blocking the way she'd come. Please, let them have made it to the other side.

It was no use hoping. First things first. She was raking the rubble-strewn floor with her torch beam, searching for Malu. The combined beam of torch and phone only reached about three feet before the dust killed it.

He must have pulled himself back.

'Malu?'

'H-here.'

A pile of stone lay between them. She was over it in seconds. It hurt, she thought vaguely. She was eight months pregnant. Climbing over loose rock, knocking rock in the process, was maybe not the wisest...

She didn't have time for wise.

He was right by the pile. He was very lucky the rocks hadn't fallen on him.

Define luck, she thought grimly, but at least he was still alive. And still conscious.

Dust and blood. A lot of it.

He had a deep gash on his thigh where his pants were ripped away. The guys had tried to tie a tourniquet but it had slipped. Blood was oozing...

But not pumping, she thought with relief. If it'd been pumping he'd be dead by now.

She was wearing a light jacket. She hauled it off, bundled it into a tight pad, placed it against the wound and pushed.

Malu screamed.

'I'm so, so sorry,' she told him, but there was no time to do anything about the pain. She had to keep pushing. 'Malu, I have drugs but I need to stop the bleeding before I do anything else. I need to press hard.'

'S-sorry. Just the shock...'

'I should have warned you.'

Go back to basics, she reminded herself, desperately fighting the need to cough, and the need to breathe through the grit. Desperately trying to sound in control. Don't start a procedure before explaining it to the patient, she reminded herself, even if she was trapped in a place that scared her witless.

Malu had relapsed into silence. She knew Malu. He

was a large, tough islander from the outermost island of the M'Langi group.

He had a wife and two small children.

She pushed harder.

She had morphine in her bag. If she had another pair of hands…

She didn't.

His pants were ripped. Yes! Still pressing with one hand, she used the other and tugged the jagged cloth. The cloth ripped almost to the ankle.

Now she was fumbling one-handed in her bag for scissors. Thank heaven she was neat. There was so much dust… Despite the torchlight she could hardly see, but the scissors were right where she always stored them.

One snip and she had the tough fabric cut at the cuff, and that gave her a length of fabric to wind. The miners had tried to use a belt as their tourniquet but it was too stiff. The torn trouser leg was a thousand times better.

She twisted and wound, tying the pad—her ex-jacket—into place. She twisted and twisted until Malu cried out again.

'Malu, the worst's over,' she told him as she somehow managed to knot it. 'The bleeding's stopped and my hands are now free. I'll make us masks to make breathing easier. Then I'll organise something to dull the pain.'

And get some fluids into you, she added to herself, saying silent prayers of thanks that she had her bag with her, that she'd had it beside her when the collapse had happened, that she'd picked it up almost automatically and that she hadn't dropped it. She had saline. She could set up a drip. But in this dust, to try and keep things sterile…

Concentrate on keeping Malu alive first, she told herself. After so much blood loss she had to replace fluids. She'd worry about bugs later.

Malu was barely responding. His pulse… *His pulse…* Get the fluids in. Move!

Five minutes later Malu had morphine on board and she had a makeshift drip feeding fluids into his arm. She'd ripped her shirt and created makeshift masks to keep the worst of the dust from their lungs. She sat back and held the saline bag up, and for the first time she thought she might have time to breathe herself.

She still felt like she was choking. Her eyes were filled with grit.

They were both alive.

'Doc?' Malu's voice was a whisper but she was onto it.

'Mmm?'

'Macca and Reuben… They were carrying me.'

'I know.'

'Reuben's my uncle. You reckon they've made it?'

'I don't know.' There was no point lying; Malu would know the risks better than she did. She grasped his hand and held. There was nothing else she could do or say.

The thought of trying to find them, trying to struggle out through the mass of rubble… Even if she could leave Malu, the thing was impossible. The rubble around them was unyielding.

Malu's hand gripped hers, hard. 'Don't even think about trying to dig out,' he muttered, and she thought that even though his words were meant as protection to her, there was more than a hint of fear for himself. To be left alone in the dark… 'It's up to them outside to do the rescuing now. Meanwhile, turn off the lights.'

'Sorry?'

'The lights. We don't need 'em. Conserve…'

'Good thinking,' she said warmly, and flicked off her torch. Then she flicked off the torch app on her phone.

But as the beam died, a message appeared on the screen. When had that come in?

She wouldn't have heard.

The message was simple.

Maddie? Tell me you're not down the mine. On way with Cairns Air Sea Rescue. Josh.

Josh.

Josh was coming.

Her phone was working. Help was on its way.

It was amazing that the signal had reached down here, but this was a shallow tunnel, with ventilation shafts rising at regular intervals. The simple knowledge that she had phone reception made her feel better. And Josh was coming... All of a sudden she felt a thousand per cent lighter. She told Malu and felt the faint relaxation of the grip on her hand. Cairns Air Sea Rescue would be the forerunners, she knew. The cavalry was heading this way.

She gripped her phone hard, as if it alone was a link to the outside world. Help. Heavy machinery. Skill, technology, care. All the things needed to get them out of here.

Josh was coming.

It shouldn't make one scrap of difference that Josh would be one of the rescue crew. Their marriage had been over for years. They talked occasionally as casual acquaintances. Friends? Probably not even that.

But still... *Josh was coming.*

'So you still got reception?' Malu whispered, sounding incredulous, and she looked at the one bar out of five signalling a really weak link to the outside world.

'Just.'

'Tell 'em to hurry,' Malu muttered. 'And tell them if

there's one single camera at the mine mouth then I need a
new pair of trousers before they bring me out.'

She even managed a chuckle. He was so brave.

His pulse was so weak…

'I'll tell them,' she said and ventured a text back.

Yeah, we're underground. There's a bit of rock between
us and the entrance. We're not very respectable. If you're
coming in we'd appreciate a change of clothes. There's a
distinct lack of laundry facilities down here.

She read it to Malu and he managed a chuckle. She
should say more, she thought. She should give a complete
medical update but for now it was enough that she was
breathing and Malu was breathing.

She just had to keep it that way until Josh…

Until the cavalry arrived.

The plane was taxiing out onto the runway. 'Phones off
now,' the pilot snapped, and Josh went to flick off his
phone—and then paused as a message appeared.

If you're coming in we'd appreciate a change of clothes.
There's a distinct lack of laundry facilities down here.

He swore. Then he swore again.

'Josh?' Beth was watching, all concern.

'She's down there,' he said grimly. 'Maddie's trapped.'

'Then all the more reason to turn your phone off so we
can take off.' But she took the phone from his hands and
stared at the screen, and her face tightened. This team were
used to horror, but when it affected one of their own…

'Wait thirty seconds,' she told the pilot, and she started
texting.

'What?' He tried to grab his phone back, but she turned her back on him and kept typing. Then the text sent, and she handed it back.

He looked down at what she'd written.

We're on our way. With Josh in the lead. He'll be in there with you, even if he has to dig in with his bare hands.

'Beth…' He could hardly speak.

'Truth?' she queried, and he tried to swallow panic. And failed.

'Truth,' he muttered, and he flicked his phone off and they were on their way.

CHAPTER TWO

WHAT BLESSED FAIRY had made her run into the mine with a fully loaded medical bag?

What bad goblin had made her run in at all?

In the hours that followed, Maddie tried to get a grip on what had happened.

There should have been systems in place to stop her, she decided as the darkness seemed to grow blacker around her. There should also have been barriers to stop the mine's ex-employees gaining access in the first place.

But who was in control? Where was Ian Lockhart? He owned this mine, or at least his brother did. So much on this island was running down. Lockhart money had dried up. There'd even been mutterings that the medical service would have to close.

At least the service had still been operating this morning, she thought, grasping at any ray of light she could find in this nightmare. The good news was that she'd been here. Yes, she'd been dumb enough to run into the mine, but she'd carried three units of saline and she'd only used two on Malu. The bleeding had slowed to nothing and his blood pressure was rising and…

And she was still trapped underground. A long way underground.

Her telephone beeped into life again. Ringing. Not a message.

A real person! But first she frantically sought settings to turn the volume down. The dust was still settling around them, and it seemed to her that any little sound might cause more rock to fall.

Malu was no longer aware. She'd given him more morphine and he'd fallen into an uneasy slumber. The ringtone hadn't woken him.

'H-hi.' It felt eerie to be calmly answering the phone in such conditions. She had to stop and cough. 'H-hold on.'

Let it be Josh.

Why did she think that? Josh was coming from Cairns. He couldn't be here yet. The coughing eased and she managed to focus again.

'Maddie?' The voice at the end of the phone was growing frantic. Not Josh.

She recognised the voice—Keanu, one of the other two island doctors. Sam, the island's chief permanent doctor, had decided to take leave before she had her baby, which meant she and Keanu were currently the only doctors on the island.

'What's happening?' he demanded. 'Are you okay?'

'We seem to be trapped but we're okay.' She glanced down again at Malu. 'You and me both, aren't we, Malu?'

Malu didn't respond but she didn't expect him to. The wound on his thigh was ugly. Without morphine he'd be writhing. She released the pressure from his makeshift mask a little, trying to get a balance between stopping the grit and making it harder for him to breathe.

Oxygen would be good. Why hadn't she lugged in an oxygen cylinder, as well?

She should have brought a wheelbarrow.

'Maddie?'

She jerked herself back to focussing on the call. 'Keanu? Malu has an impact injury, thigh.' She suspected broken ribs, possible internal injuries as well, but it was no use saying that in Malu's hearing. 'I suspect he'll need surgery when we get out of here, evac to Cairns, but I've stopped the bleeding and he's stable. Two litres of saline, five milligrams of intravenous morph…'

'You had that stuff down there?' He sounded incredulous.

'I was a girl scout,' she said dryly. 'I'm prepared.'

There was a moment's silence. Then…

'Are Macca and Reuben with you?'

'They ran when the second collapse came. They're not with us now.'

He must have her on speaker phone. She could hear sobbing in the background. He'd be in the operations room of the mine, she thought. The sobbing would be Macca's and Reuben's families.

Malu's family would be there, too.

No one belonging to her.

But then…Josh was coming. He'd said he would.

Josh wasn't her family, she reminded herself. In truth, he never had been.

'That last rockfall…' She was almost afraid to ask, but she had to. 'Was anyone else hurt?'

'Everyone's clear but you four.'

'Kalifa?'

'Maddie, worry about yourself.'

'Should I worry?'

There was a moment's silence.

'It might take a while to reach you,' Keanu said at last. 'How's the air down there?'

'Dusty.'

'But?'

'But otherwise okay.' She sniffed. 'I can feel a bit of a draught. Do you reckon there might be some sort of escape hatch?'

'It's probably from a ventilation shaft. Thank God that's still working.' He hesitated. 'Maddie, we need to bring experts and machinery from the mainland.'

'The mainland... Cairns.'

'Yep.'

'Is that coming on the mercy flight?'

'How do you know about the mercy flight?'

'Josh told me.'

There was another silence. 'Your Josh,' he said at last.

'He's not my Josh.' And then... 'How do you know he's *my* Josh?'

'Hettie told me. She relayed the message from Cairns Air Sea Rescue. But... You've been talking to him yourself?'

'Yes.'

'Maddie?'

'Mmm?'

'You need to conserve your phone. It's probably not the time for chats with your ex.'

'He texted. I also have three battery backups in my bag. That's enough for two days.'

'That might not be enough.'

'You have to be kidding.'

'I hope I am,' he said. 'But for now...two days or not, conserve your phone.'

Two days or not, conserve your phone.

Maddie sat back on her heels and tried—really hard—not to panic.

Two days?

There'd been an incident, not so long ago, where miners had been trapped…where? Tasmania? The miners had been successfully brought to the surface after how many days? Fourteen? She couldn't remember the details but she remembered watching the rescue unfold on television. She'd been mesmerised by the tragedy of the mine collapse but even more mesmerised by the courage shown by the miners trying to keep their sanity as the appalling endurance test had stretched on.

Neither of them had been badly injured.

Malu was suffering from shock and a deep laceration, she thought, but what else? She wanted X-rays. She wanted him in hospital. She wanted a sterile environment and the necessary surgery for his leg.

She couldn't even see him.

Two days…

The darkness was absolute.

Her fingers were on Malu's wrist. His pulse was settling. There was no need to turn on the torch.

She flicked the torch on anyway, just for a moment. Just to see.

Their chamber was about eight feet in diameter. The roof was still up there, and there were shoring timbers above them. Where their tiny enclosure ended, the shoring timbers had splintered like kindling.

The floor was rock-strewn. She needed to clear it a bit to get Malu more comfortable.

She could do it without the torch. She had to do it without the torch. She flicked it off again and the total darkness was like a physical slap.

Her phone gave a tiny ping and the screen lit momentarily. She took three deep breaths—because she had been close to panic—and she let herself look.

Landed. You nice and safe down there? Got a couple of good rocks you can use for pillows or are you thinking you might like to come on up? Josh.

She could have kissed him. Except she didn't kiss Josh. Not any more. He'd always been uncomfortable with overt displays of affection. Even when they'd been married… Affection had been an effort, she thought, seizing on the excuse to get her mind off the dust. She'd never been in any doubt that he'd wanted her, but affection had been for behind closed doors. It was almost as if he'd been ashamed to admit he'd needed her.

He didn't need her. He'd figured that five years ago when he'd walked away from their marriage. But right now she needed him. She texted him.

I'm not going anywhere. Just trying to decide which rock pillow to use. It seems I have a choice. Have given Malu morphine. He's suffered major blood loss. Have given two litres of saline. I only have one more and want to hold it in reserve.

For drinking? She didn't say it. She couldn't.

Heart rate a hundred and twenty. Only just conscious. Worrying.

Damn Keanu and his ban on using her phone, she decided, as she hit Send. Okay, her battery life was precious, but Josh was a trauma specialist, a good one, and she needed advice. If she was going to be stuck down here with Malu, then the least she could do was keep him alive.

Which meant texting Josh. Didn't it?

She didn't get the little whoosh as her message sent.

She stared at the single flickering bar of reception on her screen and willed it to send. Send. *Send.*

The screen went blank again and she was left with darkness.

Whoosh.

Sent. Delivered. At least she hoped it had been delivered. Josh would be on his way from Wildfire's tiny airstrip, and he had to cross the mountains to get to the mine. There were places up there where there was no phone reception at all.

How long before he saw it?

Did it matter? She was pretty sure there was nothing more she could do medically for Malu, except make him comfortable.

Comfortable? Rock pillows. Ha!

Josh will text when he can, she told herself, and the thought was comforting.

Why? Why Josh rather than anyone else?

She had lots of friends on Wildfire Island. She'd been working as a fly in, fly out doctor here for five years now, spending two weeks here, one week in Cairns. She was doing okay. She'd put her marriage behind her. This next stage of her life… Well, it was a gamble but it was something—someone—she desperately wanted.

Unconsciously her hand went to her belly. She'd been hit as the rocks had flown, but surely she'd protected her baby enough?

Why on earth had she risked her baby? It had been a split-second decision but now…it seemed almost criminally stupid.

'I'm sorry. I'm so sorry,' she whispered to the little one in her belly, and she felt like weeping.

She had to talk to someone.

Maybe she could text Hettie. Hettie, Wildfire's charge

nurse administrator, was a real friend, whereas Josh was now merely a contact, someone she'd put to the back of her mind like she'd put old school photos to the back of her wardrobe. One day she'd throw them out.

But not yet, she decided as she told herself she couldn't phone anyone and started groping her way around the floor. She was shoving loose rocks to the side, clearing space so she could make Malu as comfortable as possible.

Photos. The thought was suddenly weirdly front and centre. Pictures of her mother before the stroke. Photographs of her wedding day.

They were all history, she told herself. She should get rid of them all. She touched her belly again, lightly, a touch that, all at once, seemed to be almost a prayer.

'I don't need any of it,' she said out loud, even though speaking was impossibly hard through the dust. 'The past is just that. I have a future now.'

But still…

Text soon, she pleaded silently to her phone. Please, Josh?

And she went on clearing rocks.

A truck met them at the airstrip. A chopper would have been more sensible, Josh thought grimly as they transferred gear from the plane to the truck, but the instructions had been explicit. 'We used to keep a solid clearing around the minehead but there's been cost-cutting,' Hettie had told them. The charge nurse at the hospital had put herself in charge of communication. 'The jungle's come back and even the parking lot got so rutted in the last rain it'd take hours to clear a landing site. We'll get you from the airstrip to the mine by truck.'

If they couldn't land the choppers, the injured would have to be trucked back to the airstrip for evacuation.

The injured…

Maddie?

The thought of where she was made Josh feel sick. He couldn't think of her. He had to concentrate on the job at hand—but it was taking too long to reach her.

To reach it. To reach the mine.

Maddie.

With the gear loaded he jumped into the front passenger seat of the lorry. Another jeep took Beth. They turned off the coast road, skirting the plateau to the other side of the island.

He checked his phone.

Nothing.

'There's no reception, mate,' the lorry driver told him. 'Not with the plateau between us and transmission.'

'Do you know anything more?'

'Not more'n you, probably.' The guy's knuckles were white on the steering wheel, but it wasn't because of hard driving. His face was grim as death. 'We haven't heard from Macca and Reuben. They're mates. We know Malu and Doc Haddon are alive but they're trapped.' The man's knuckles gripped even tighter. 'Bloody Lockhart. Rips all the money from the mine and what does he do with it? He's been told those shoring timbers needed replacing or the mine sealed. And where is he? Not here facing what he's done, that's for sure. It won't be him crawling down the mine trying to get them out.'

'That'll be Max Lockhart?' Josh ventured, trying not to think of anyone crawling down the mine to get…Maddie out. He was dredging up stuff he'd seen in the press about this island group. 'Isn't Max Lockhart the owner of Wildfire?'

'Yeah.' The guy spat out the window of the moving truck. 'But we've hardly seen hide nor hair of Max for years. Ian's his brother. He took over day-to-day running of the mine a few years back. He's supposed to be running the island for his brother, but as far as we can see he's just out for what he can get. He's somewhere overseas now. The mine got dangerous, the money stopped and he left. And now this mess... How the hell are we going to get 'em out?' There was a moment's silence and then he swore with an intensity Josh had never heard before and never wanted to hear again.

'And... Doc Haddon?' Josh ventured, not because he wanted to but because he was almost forced to say it.

The knuckles kept their death grip but the lines on the man's face softened. 'She's a great kid. Well, maybe she's not a kid any more but I'm sixty, mate, so she's a kid to me. She's been on the island for five years now. The wife got shingles last year. Doc saw her in the market, saw the bumps. We'd thought they were just bites but before we knew it Doc had her at the clinic. She gave her this fancy medicine right on the spot. The shingles was bad enough but Ally—that's our daughter—she looked it up on the internet and said if Mum hadn't taken the stuff it could have been ten times worse. And every day Doc found an excuse to pop in. When she was off island she got Caroline or Ana to come instead. You know that nerve pain they get? Real bad, it was, but Doc Maddie was right onto it. She cares for everyone like that.'

And then his face hardened again. 'They say she just ran in. Everyone else was running out and someone shouted that Malu was bleeding so hard the guys carrying him had to stop. She grabbed her bag and ran. She's a hero.'

And his voice cracked with emotion as he swiped his arm across his face and sniffed.

Josh's phone pinged. He glanced down, trying not to hope, but the word on his screen read *Maddie*.

He couldn't read the message. For some dumb reason his eyes were blurry, too. He had to do a matching swipe before he could make it out.

I'm not going anywhere. Just trying to decide which rock pillow to use. It seems I have a choice. Have given Malu morphine. He's suffered major blood loss. Have given two litres of saline. I only have one more and want to hold it in reserve. Heart rate a hundred and twenty. Only just conscious. Worrying.

How long since that'd been sent? While he was in the air? He swiped his face again and turned into doctor. Texted back, hoping whatever sliver of reception he had would last.

You're doing great. Heart rate will be high considering shock. Do what you can to keep him warm, cuddle him if you need to. If it's his thigh, see if you can get him sloped so his legs are higher than his heart. But you know this, Maddie. Trust your instincts. Love you.

And then he paused.

How many times in the past had he texted his wife and finished with the words *Love you*?

'You've never really loved me.' He remembered Maddie saying it to him in those last dreadful days when he'd known their marriage was over. 'Love shares, Josh. Love gives and takes and you don't know how.'

Love you?

She was right, of course. He hadn't loved her. Or not enough.

He stared at the screen for a moment and then he deleted some characters. Then hit Send. Without the love.

'I can't imagine what the wives are going through,' the truck driver said, almost to himself. 'And Pearl... Malu's wife... She's another who thinks the sun rises and sets with Maddie. Y'know, our local mums are supposed to go to Cairns six weeks before bubs are born but the docs can't make 'em so Pearl didn't. Maddie had to be choppered out to Atangi in the middle of the night. Breech it was, and Doc Maddie did an emergency Caesarean, right there in Pearl's kitchen. Pearl won't go to any other doctor since. And now Doc's trapped with Malu. Doesn't bear thinking of.'

Josh tried to think of something to say—and couldn't. He didn't trust his own voice.

'Married yourself, are you?' the guy asked at last. They were heading downhill now, through dense tropical rainforest, presumably towards the coast. Josh was trying to consider the terrain, thinking of what he already knew: that the rainforest had reclaimed most of the cleared land round the minehead, and how hard it was going to be to get machinery in.

He wanted to worry about machinery. About technicalities. He wanted to worry about anything but Maddie.

Married yourself? The guy's question still hung.

'No,' he said at last. 'Not now.'

He didn't deserve to be married. He hadn't protected... He'd failed.

Born to useless, drug-addicted parents, Josh had been the protector since he could first remember. The strong one.

He remembered a social worker, one of the early ones, walking into their house to find Holly curled on the bed and whimpering. There hadn't been food in the house for days.

He'd been eight and Holly five. Josh had been big for his

age, confused, helpless, as hungry as his little sister, but he hadn't been whimpering. He'd learned early not to cry.

And the woman had turned on him, shocked into an automatic attack. 'Why didn't you come for help?' she'd demanded. 'You're big enough now to protect your sister. Why didn't you at least tell a neighbour?'

He'd never made that mistake again. He'd protected and protected and protected—but it hadn't worked. He remembered the helplessness of being torn apart from Holly, placed in separate foster homes. The nightmares.

He'd learned to disguise even those. His job was to protect, not to share his pain. Not to add to that hurt.

And now? Once again Maddie was hurting and he was stuck on the far side of a mountain.

'Partner?' Maybe the guy was trying to distract himself. Surely he was. They were his friends underground.

And that was what Maddie was, he told himself. His friend. Nothing more.

'I guess... A girlfriend,' he told the guy and tried to think of Karen. They'd only been dating for three months but that was practically long-term for Josh. Karen was fun and flirty and out for a good time. She didn't mind that his job took him away so much. She used him as he used her— as an appendage for weddings and the like, and someone to have fun with when it suited them both.

Maybe she wasn't even a girlfriend, Josh thought. But that didn't matter.

Whereas Maddie...

'Here we are,' the truck driver said, turning off the main road—if you could call it a main road—into a fenced-off area. The main gates were wide open. The sign on the fence said Mining Area—Keep Out, but there was no trace of security.

There were a few dilapidated buildings nestled among

the trees. Only the cluster of parked vehicles, an ancient fire truck, a police motorbike and a jeep with the Wildfire Medical insignia, told him that anything was wrong.

'Best place for the chopper's round the back,' the truck driver told him. 'The guys were starting to clear it when we left.' He pulled to a halt outside the first of the buildings and turned and clamped a hand on Josh's shoulder. 'Good luck, mate,' he told him. 'Thanks for coming. We sure need you.'

Josh climbed out of the truck and as he did his phone pinged. Maddie again.

We're warm enough. Could use a bit of air-conditioning. Do you think you could arrange it? Also a couple of fluffy pillows, two mattresses and Malu reckons he could handle a beer. I could handle a gin and tonic, though I suppose I'm stuck with a lemonade. Actually lemonade sounds brilliant. I'm happy to make do. That's my 'needs' list, Dr Campbell. Could you get onto it, stat?

A pillow would be nice. A pillow would be magnificent. Instead, Maddie lay on her back, with her hands behind her head, trying not to think how hard the rock was. And how much of a dead weight Malu's legs were.

See if you can get him sloped so his legs are higher than his heart.

That was easier said than done. She could have put rocks under his thighs—yeah, that'd be comfy. Instead, she'd emptied her soft leather medical bag and given that to him as a pillow. She'd given him a couple of sips of the water—not as much as he wanted but she was starting to figure that if Keanu said two days then she might need to ration. Then, out of options, she'd lain down and lifted his legs onto hers.

It helped. She had her hand on his wrist and she could feel the difference.

He'd objected but not very much. In truth, he was drifting in and out of consciousness. He could hardly assess what she was doing.

She wouldn't mind a bit of unconsciousness herself. She ached where she'd been hit by flying debris. She had a scratch on her head. Blood had trickled down and it was sticky. And grimy.

She'd kill for a wash.

Her back hurt.

Cramps?

That was her imagination, she told herself fiercely. It had to be.

Lie still and think of England.

Think of Josh? He's out there.

Josh. Her husband.

He was no such thing, she told herself, but for now, in the dust and grit, she allowed herself to think it. She'd married him. She'd made vows and she'd meant them.

When she'd signed the divorce papers it'd broken her heart.

'Josh…' She couldn't help herself. She said his name aloud, like it was some sort of talisman. She didn't need him, or at least she hadn't needed him until now. Josh hated to be needed.

But that wasn't true, she conceded. He loved to be physically needed, like he was needed now, flying off to the world's emergencies, doctor in crisis, doing what he could to help in the worst possible situations. But when she'd needed to share emotional pain?

That's when he'd been…divorced.

'Who's Josh?'

Malu asked his question sleepily. He stirred, winced, swore then settled again. His legs were so heavy. She couldn't do this for much longer, she decided, but she'd cope as long as she could.

'Josh is my ex-husband,' she said, more to distract herself than anything else. Doctors didn't reveal their personal lives to their patients, yet down here the lines between professional and personal were blurred. Two days? Please not.

'He's a trauma specialist with Cairns Air Sea Rescue,' she said, and the words seemed a comfort all by themselves. 'He's texted. He's on his way.

'Because of you?' Malu's words were slurred, but strong enough to reassure her.

'It's his job.'

'So not because of you.'

'We've been divorced for five years.'

'Yeah?' Malu must be using this as a means to distract himself from the pain, from the fear, from the difficulty breathing, she decided. It was so hard to talk through the dust.

She couldn't tell him to hush and conserve his energy. Maybe she needed distraction, too.

'So he's not the dad?' Malu asked.

'No.' She wasn't going there and it seemed Malu sensed it.

'I can't imagine being divorced from my Pearl,' Malu managed, moving on. 'So…five years ago? What happened? Wrong guy in the first place? He play fast and loose?'

'I guess…first option. He was always the wrong guy.' She thought about it for a bit and then suddenly she found herself talking. Talking about Josh. Talking, as she'd never spoken of it to anyone.

'Josh had it tough,' she said, softly into the dark. 'He had a younger sister, Holly. His parents were worse than useless and that the two of them survived at all was a miracle. They were abandoned as kids and went from foster home to foster home. Sometimes they were separated but Josh fought battle after battle to keep them together. To keep his sister safe. Their only constant was each other.'

'B-bummer...'

'Yeah,' she said softly. 'It was a bummer. But Josh was tough. He got a scholarship and made it into medicine, then worked his way through university, supporting Holly while he did it.'

'Where'd you meet him?'

'Just after I finished university. I was a first-year intern. We became friends and...well, one thing led to another.'

'To marriage.'

'That's right,' she whispered, thinking back to the precious months before that nightmare time. Lying in the dark, holding Josh. Feeling him hold her. Feeling his love unfold, feeling that they might have a chance.

'B-but?' He coughed and coughed again and then moaned, and she did a recalculation of morphine dosages and figured she could give him more in half an hour. She daren't give it sooner. She couldn't drug him too deeply, not with this amount of dust in the air.

So distract him. Tell him...the truth?

'I'm still not sure the reasons for marriage were solid,' she told him. 'My mum...well, maybe you already know? I told Pearl about her when she asked why I don't stay on Wildfire all the time. My dad took off when I was six. I'm an only child. We were incredibly close—and then she had a stroke. Major. She's unable to do anything for herself. She's permanently damaged. Anyway, as I said, Josh was my colleague and my friend, and when the stroke happened he was amazing. He cared for me when I was gutted. He cared for Mum—in fact, I think sometimes he still visits her. He did…everything right. And I thought…well, I fell so deeply in love I found myself pregnant.'

'Hey, that happens,' Malu whispered. 'Like me 'n Pearl. Never a better thing, though. So, your Josh. He was happy about it?'

'I'm not sure,' she whispered. 'He told me he was. But there's one thing Josh is good at, and that's hiding his emotions. All I knew was that he seemed happy about the baby, and he said he loved me. So we married. He still felt a bit…distant but I thought…maybe…'

'So what happened to the baby? What broke you up?'

'Knowledge,' she said bleakly. 'Learning Josh knows how to care, but not to share. Do you really want to listen to this?'

'Pearl says I'm a gossip,' Malu whispered, and grabbed her hand and held on. A link in the darkness. 'Tell me.' And then, as she hesitated, his grip tightened. 'I know it's not my business, but honest, Maddie, I'm scared. You could tell me it's all going to be fine but we both know that's not true. Distract me. Anything that's said in the mine stays in the mine.'

She almost smiled. 'That seems a really good arm twist to give you more gossip.'

She sensed a half smile in return. She was friends with his wife, but she barely knew Malu. Though maybe that was no longer true, she decided. There was nothing like hurling you down a mine and locking you in, with the threat of rockfalls real and constant, to make you know someone really fast.

And what harm to talk about Josh now? she asked herself. Somewhere he was out there, worrying. Caring. Caring was what he was good at, she thought.

Caring wasn't enough.

Tell Malu? She might as well. He needed distraction and she…well, so did she.

'They say troubles come in threes,' she said finally into the dark. 'So did ours. Mum had her stroke. We got married, which was the good bit, but there were two more tragedies waiting in the wings. We lost the baby—Mikey was born prematurely—and then Josh's little sister died.'

'Oh, Maddie.' What sort of doctor–patient relationship was this? she asked herself. It was Malu doing the comforting.

As Josh had comforted.

'You know, if it had been my sister and only my baby, like it was my mum, I'm guessing Josh would have coped brilliantly,' she said, and now she was almost speaking to herself. Sorting it out in her mind. 'But it was Josh's pain and he didn't know how to cope with it. It left him gutted and his reaction was to stonewall himself. He just emotionally disappeared.'

'How can you do that?'

'Normal people can't,' Maddie said slowly. 'But Josh had one hell of a childhood. He never talks about it but when I met him his sister was doing brilliantly, at uni herself, happy and bubbly. She told me how bad it had been but Josh never did. He used to have nightmares but when I woke him he'd never tell me what they were about. Sometimes I'd wake and hear him pacing in the night and I knew there were demons. And then came baby Mikey, too small to live. And Holly. One drunk driver, a car mounting the footpath. So after all that, Josh's care came to nothing and he went so far into himself I couldn't reach him. He finally explained to me, quite calmly, that he couldn't handle himself. He didn't know how to be a husband to me any more. He had to leave.'

She shook her head, trying to shake off the memory of the night Josh had finally declared their marriage was over.

There was a long silence, for which she was grateful. And then she thought...

These *are* cramps. Stomach cramps.

Back cramps?

And that thought brought a stab of fear so deep it terrified her.

She was lying on a rock floor, supporting Malu's legs. Of course she had cramps.

Of course?

Please...

'I can top up the morphine now if you like,' she managed at last, and at least this was an excuse to turn on the torch. She needed the phone app torch, too, to clean the dust away and inject the morphine. She held the phone for a bit too long after.

The light was a comfort.

The phone would be better.

No word. No texting.

Cramps.

Josh...

Malu's grip on her hand gradually lessened. She thought he was drifting into sleep, but maybe the rocks were too hard. The morphine didn't cut it.

'So your Josh abandoned you and joined Cairns Air Sea Rescue?' he whispered at last.

Oh, her back hurt. She wouldn't mind some of that morphine herself...

Talk, she told herself. Don't think of anything but distracting Malu.

'I think that other people's trauma, other people's pain, are things he can deal with,' she managed, struggling to find the right words. Struggling to find the right answer.

'But losing our baby… It hurt him to look at me hurting, and when Holly died, he didn't know where to put himself. He couldn't comfort me and he thought showing me his pain would make mine worse. He couldn't help me, so he left.'

'Oh, girl…'

'I'm fine,' she whispered, and Malu coughed again and then gripped tighter.

'I dunno much,' he wheezed. 'But I do know I'm very sure you're not.'

'Not what?'

'Fine. You're hurting and it's not just the memory of some low-life husband walking out on you.'

'I'm okay.'

'I can tell pain when I hear it.'

'I got hit by a few rocks. We both have bruises all over.'

'There's room on my pillow to share.'

'It's not exactly professional—to share my patient's bed.'

'I'm just sharing the pillow,' Malu told her with an attempt at laughter. 'You have to provide your own rock base.'

She tried to smile. Her phone pinged and she'd never read a text message faster.

Hey, you. Quick update? Tell us you're okay. Josh.

'Is that telling us the bulldozers are coming?' Malu demanded, and the threadiness of his voice had her switching on the torch again. 'Hey, it's okay,' he managed. 'You tell them…tell them to tell Pearl I'm okay. But I wouldn't mind a bulldozer.'

'I wouldn't mind a piece of foam,' she told him, and tried to think of what to say to Josh. Apart from the fact that she was scared. No, make that terrified. She hated the dark and she was starting to panic and the dust in her lungs made it hard to breathe and the cramps...

Get a grip. Hysterics were no use to anyone.

She shouldn't have come in in the first place, she told herself.

Yeah, and then Malu would be dead.

Josh wanted facts. He couldn't cope with emotion.

Yeah, Josh, we're fine.

CHAPTER THREE

JOSH WASN'T ON Wildfire to dig into a mine and pull people out. Not even Maddie. Josh was there to assess medical need, perform triage, arrange evacuation where possible and then get his hands dirty dealing with injuries needing on-the-ground treatment.

And there was a need. The locals were doing all they could, but the medical team here consisted of one doctor and two nurses. It had apparently taken the doctor—an islander called Keanu—time to get there, and the guy who had been injured first was taking up his attention. A fractured leg followed by a cardiac arrest left room for little else.

But there was more medical need. Apparently, before Keanu had arrived, the miners had fought their way back into mine, frantically trying to reach their injured mates. It hadn't worked. There'd been a further cave-in. Further casualties. Keanu barely had time to acknowledge Josh and Beth's arrival.

There was still a sense of chaos. Keanu had ordered everyone back from the mine mouth but no one seemed to be in charge of rescue efforts.

'Where's the mine manager?' Josh snapped as he surveyed the scene before him. A group of filthy miners were huddled at the mouth of the mine, with pretty much matching expressions of shock and loss. Keanu had organised the casualties a little way away, under the shade of palm trees. He and the nurses were working frantically over the guy with the injured leg, but he shook his head as Josh approached.

'We have everything we need here. It's touch and go for this guy and there's others needing help. The guy with the arm first.' He motioned across to where a miner was on the ground, his mate beside him.

'No breathing problems?'

'They've all had a lungful of rock—we could use a tank of oxygen—but...'

'I'll get Beth to do a respiratory assessment. Beth?'

'Onto it.' She was already heading for the truck, for oxygen canisters. 'Okay, guys,' she called. 'Anyone want a face wipe and a whiff of something that'll do you good? Line up here.'

'What's happening down the mine?' Josh asked.

'Hettie's called the mining authorities in Cairns. We need expertise. They're sending engineers and equipment now.'

From Cairns. It'd take hours.

Maddie was down there.

Keanu was adjusting a drip, watching the guy's breathing like an eagle watched a mouse. A tiny thing, the rise and fall of a chest, but so important. 'So you're the ex-husband,' he managed.

'Yeah.'

'Yeah, well, we all love Maddie, but she's in there now and it's up to the experts to get her out. Meanwhile, sorry, mate, but there's more work here than we can handle. We're still trying to stabilise. We have a suspected ruptured spleen, a guy with an arm so crushed he might lose it, a fractured leg with shock and breathing problems and more. Could you look at the spleen for me?'

And somehow Josh had to stop thinking of Maddie underground, Maddie trapped, Maddie deep in a mine where there'd already been two major rockfalls. He needed to focus on the here and now.

Triage…

He headed across to the guy with the suspected ruptured spleen. As long as he wasn't going into shock—which he could be if the rupture was significant—then the arm was the first priority. If he could save it.

Four underground. Including Maddie.

'Who's the mine manager?' he snapped, asking it not of Keanu, who was committed to the patient under his hands, but of the miners in general.

'Ian Lockhart,' one of the men ventured. 'At least, he's supposed to be in charge but he lit out when the debt collectors started sniffing around.'

'Was he in charge of day-to-day running of the mine?'

'That used to be Pete Blake. Max Lockhart owns the island but he's never here. He put Pete in charge but Ian reckoned he knew it all. He sacked Pete last year and took over the day-to-day stuff himself. Reuben Alaki's acting supervisor now but…' He hesitated and his voice cracked. 'Reuben's one of the guys stuck down there.'

'Is Pete still on the island?'

'He'll probably be out fishing.'

'Get him,' Josh snapped. 'Use one of the island choppers to bring him here—do an air drop.'

'What, pluck him off his boat and drop him here?'

'Exactly,' Josh snapped. 'We need expertise now.' He bent over the guy with the fractured arm. Compound. Messy. 'Okay, mate, let's get you assessed and see if we can do something for the pain. Meanwhile let's get things moving to get your mates out from underground.'

And then a nose wedged its way under his arm and he almost froze with shock. It was a great, bounding golden retriever.

Bugsy.

It was so long since he'd seen the dog it was all he could do not to shed a few tears into his shaggy coat. The big dog recognised him. That was amazing all by itself.

He'd given Bugsy to Maddie after their honeymoon, just before he'd gone back to work. His job was search and rescue. He spent days at a time in remote places, coping with emergencies like this one.

He'd been aware just how alone Maddie had been— that was one of the reasons he'd married her. Puppy Bugsy had been a great idea. He'd been their one constant when things had fallen apart, but when things had really fallen apart it had been logical that Maddie take him.

That he was here... On the island...

He couldn't focus on the dog, though. The fracture was severe. On first assessment he thought enough blood was getting through to keep the hand viable, but suddenly... it wasn't.

And behind him Keanu had the CPR unit set up on the guy with the fractured leg.

'Go find Maddie,' he said to Bugsy, pushing the great head away with a wrench that almost physically hurt. 'I can't go to her but maybe... Go fetch Maddie. Go!'

The cramping was hurting. Really hurting.

It's only my back, she told herself. It has to be only my back. I must have wrenched it when I fell.

The cramps were fifteen minutes apart...

Or more like ten.

Uh-oh.

* * *

'Josh, I need you here.'

Keanu wouldn't be calling if the need wasn't beyond urgent. He elevated the arm he'd been treating and called for Beth to hold it steady, as straight as possible. Please, let enough blood get through to keep it viable until he got back. The man needed two of him.

At least it stopped him thinking about Maddie.

'So tell me how you met Pearl?'

Malu might be her patient, Maddie thought, but the distinction between doctor and patient was getting blurred. The blackness was closing in, and her only link to reality seemed to be Malu's hand. But it was she who was doing the comforting, she told herself. Of course it was.

She'd asked the question to distract him from pain and fear. And she needed him to answer, because she needed to be distracted from pain and fear right back.

So she listened as, in a faltering voice that sometimes paused for long enough to make her worry, Malu told of growing up on the island, of diving, of fishing, of learning to show off to the girls.

Of being in sixth grade and kicking a ball between the desks with his mates. Of being punished by being made to sit next to a girl.

Of watching Pearl write a story about watching the boys dive, then listening to the teacher praise it and saying, 'You boys might dive any time you can, but by writing it down, Pearl keeps it forever.'

Of deciding right there and then that she was his woman.

Of it taking ten years before she finally agreed.

Then babies. Domestic drama. Love…

Maddie was blinking as Malu's voice finally trailed off and she realised he'd drifted into sleep.

Love, she thought. You didn't realise how rare it was until you lost it.

She'd lost her baby. Born so prematurely... Mikey. He'd lived for two hours.

And she'd lost Josh.

Actually, she hadn't lost him, she told herself harshly. She'd never had him. And now she had a baby to love on her own.

She'd brought her baby into a collapsed mine. How could she have done something so stupid? Even to save Malu... To risk her baby...

Josh was out there, she told herself, and, as if on cue, her phone rang.

It rang, didn't ping for an incoming message, and when she answered, miraculously it was Josh!

'Hi!'

Do not cry, she told herself. *You will not.*

'Maddie?'

She took a couple of deep breaths—or as deep as she could manage—and tried to talk.

'J-Josh.'

'Hey...'

'No. Sorry. I'm scaring you.' She was fighting to get a grip, immensely grateful that Malu was sleeping. 'There's nothing to scare you for. Malu's settling. His blood pressure's rising. I think we can manage without the third bag of saline.' No need to mention why she wanted to hold it in reserve. 'Raising his legs seems to have helped. I've given him an additional five milligrams of morphine. He's... We're as good as we can be.' And then she cracked, just a little. 'Any idea when we might expect help?'

'We're working on it. Pete Blake's just been choppered

in. He was out on the reef, fishing. He knows the old seams backwards.'

'P-Pete's good.' He was, too. She—and the rest of the islanders—had been appalled when he'd been sacked. 'But…'

'But he can't get you out on his own,' Josh told her. 'There needs to be careful appraisal before we do anything. I think you need to face staying where you are overnight.'

Overnight. Right. At least that was better than Keanu's two days.

'How will we know it's bedtime?' she managed, striving for lightness.

'The time will be on your phone, Maddie, but I'll ring you and tell you anyway. If you like, I'll even sing you a lullaby.'

'You!'

'My voice is improving with age,' he said, sounding wounded. 'You want to hear?'

'No!'

'No taste,' he said mournfully. 'I don't know why I married you.'

'I don't know, either,' she said, and suddenly it was serious again. The past was flooding back—but also the present. 'Josh?'

'Mmm?'

'What's happening out there?'

'We've just saved a hand.'

She drew in her breath. 'Whose?'

'Max Stubbs.'

'Oh!' She thought back, remembering the stream of miners emerging from the mine mouth. Max had been there, staggering but on his feet. 'His blood supply was compromised? I missed it.'

'You're going to blame yourself?'

'If I'd stayed on top…'

'You made a call. Malu's need was greater.'

'I didn't even assess…'

'It wasn't compromised when you saw it. It was an unstable fracture and it moved. It's okay. We got it in time.'

She hesitated but she really wanted to know. 'What else did I miss?'

'Nothing.'

'Then why the sag in your voice? What aren't you telling me?' She knew this guy. He hid his emotions, but not well enough. Maybe that was why he'd had to walk away from her; because somehow she'd seen behind the wall.

'Maddie…'

'If you don't tell me I'll assume there's some sort of gas leak and it's on its way in here now, creeping in, inch by inch, ready to swallow—'

'Maddie!'

'So tell me!'

He hesitated again, but finally conceded. 'We lost a patient. The first guy out.'

'Kalifa?' She was incredulous. 'He had a broken leg.'

'Cardiac arrest. Sixty-seven years old. Overweight. He should never have been down the mine in the first place.'

'None of them should,' she said bitterly. 'But Kalifa… His heart… Oh, no. I should have—'

'Cut yourself some slack,' he said curtly. 'You were one doctor in the middle of a disaster. You did what you could. There were a couple more injuries from guys trying to be heroes after you disappeared but we're thinking they'll be fine. How's the battery on the phone?'

Her battery was okay. It had to be. This link to Josh seemed the only thing keeping her sane. 'I have backup but I'll be careful. Josh?'

'Mmm?'

'You need to go back to work.'

'I do. We're stabilising, then we'll get everyone we can to the hospital here or out to Cairns. But I'll be staying at the mine mouth.'

Why did that make her feel a thousand times better? Why did his voice make something inside her settle, something that had been unsettled for years?

'Bugsy's been here,' he said tangentially. 'I saw him when I first got here. How come you get to keep him on the island when you're fly in, fly out?'

'He's become our hospital dog. Everyone loves him, but officially Hettie looks after him when I'm in Cairns. Hettie's our nurse administrator. She's tough on the outside, marshmallow on the inside.'

'Like me,' Josh said, and she heard his smile and why it made her want to weep again she didn't know.

Still that strange feeling. But she was over Josh, she told herself. She had to be.

'You're okay?' he demanded, and she struggled to make herself sound okay. The cramps... The pain in her back... But what was the point of worrying him? It wasn't like he could wave a magic wand and get her out of here.

'I'm fine.'

'You don't sound fine.'

'Okay, I'm sure my lipstick's smudged but I can't find a mirror.'

She heard him chuckle, but she knew the chuckle was forced. 'I'll ring you again in an hour, if Keanu's not watching,' he promised, and she managed to smile, and managed to tell herself the cramps weren't bad and she wasn't going to cry and she didn't need Josh here, now, holding her.

'And if he is?' she managed.

'I'll ring you anyway. I promise.'

* * *

She was trying not to think of Josh. She was also trying not to think of contra—of cramps. If she lay very still the cramps weren't so bad.

If only they weren't so regular.

They were every ten minutes or so, sweeping through her entire body. She had to fight not to gasp. Not to cry out.

If I lie very still…

She lay very still.

She lay in the dark and stared at nothing and her hands cradled the swell of her belly.

'I'm so sorry,' she whispered. 'I should have thought of you first.'

'Maddie…'

'Mmm?' Malu was stirring.

'Time for another of those wee jabs?'

'Pain scale, one to ten?' she asked, and he thought about it.

'Eight,' he said at last. 'And you?'

'I'm not—'

'Lying? I'm damned sure you are. You want to take your legs out from under mine?'

'No, I—'

'Or I'll shift 'em myself.'

'Malu…'

'There's two of us in this mess,' he said morosely. 'We keep things fair.' And then he hesitated. 'Though that's not true, is it? There's three.'

'Don't…'

'You are hurting. I can hear it in your breathing.'

'I told you, I got bumped.'

'How many weeks are you?'

'I… Thirty-four.' She was lying. Stupid, stupid, stupid. She'd gambled and she'd lost, big time.

Not catastrophically, though, she pleaded. Please…
'Maddie!'

'It's okay,' she managed. 'We just need to be patient.
You want another sip of water?'

'Yeah.' But there was a world of meaning in that word.
A sip… What they both wanted was a river. Or six.

'Pearl says you don't know who the daddy is.'

'Leave it, Malu.'

'You don't want to talk about it?'

'I don't want to think about it.' She'd just got through
another cramp and her fear was building by the minute.
'I don't want to think about it at all.'

'No one's going near the mine until the engineers arrive
from Cairns.' Pete, the sacked mine manager, had been
lowered by chopper. He was still in his fishing gear and
smelled of bait, but he was competent and authoritative. He
was also adamant. 'The seam they're in…well, suicidal's
not the word for it. Even Lockhart… He was greedy for
every ounce of gold the mine'd give him. He knew it was
a rich seam but the ground's unstable granite. Burrowing into it's like burrowing into rocky sand. It's a miracle
the shoring timbers have stayed up as long as they have.'

'But we have two alive and two don't-knows in there,'
Josh said bleakly. 'How—?'

'We worry about getting them out when the engineers
arrive.' Pete was standing in front of the mine entrance
and his body language said that anyone who wanted to go
in there had to go through him. Which would maybe take
a bulldozer. 'But initially we can check the ventilation
shafts. There's a possibility we might be able to get lines
through, enough to check air supply and to get them water.'

While they waited for rescue that might never happen?
That might be too dangerous to even consider? The words

were left unsaid but they didn't have to be said. They were so loud in Josh's head that everything else seemed muted.

The initial rush of trauma-related work had abated. The guys with the fractured arm and the suspected ruptured spleen were on their way to the airstrip, and then to Cairns. A doctor who'd been conducting research out on Atangi had been on the fishing boat with Pete. He'd agreed to fly back to Cairns as acting medical officer.

That was Josh's job, but Josh wasn't moving. Instead, he was pacing, like a trapped, caged animal with nowhere to go.

There was nothing to do.

Engineers were due to arrive at any minute. They had another couple of hours of daylight.

How much air was down the mine? How to get fluids down?

And then there was a shout.

'Hey, someone's down there. Someone's coming up.'

There was a surge towards the mine entrance but Pete was still in blocking mode. He spread his arms so no one could get past him—and then Pete saw who it was and forgot about security, making a surge himself.

And two minutes later he was helping Macca support Reuben for the last few yards. As the dust cleared, and the surge of miners parted, Josh got a clear view. Two miners, both islanders. An older man, in his fifties, staggering, dragging a leg behind him. A younger guy, tall, filthy, supporting his mate.

The younger guy's hand holding... Bugsy. Maddie's dog. Though it was kind of hard to tell—the usually gold of the retriever's coat was now matted black.

The big dog was wagging his tail, but even as Josh watched him he tugged sideways, looking back at the mine entrance.

'Hold, Bugsy,' he snapped. He was fifty yards away and he could see exactly what the dog intended to do.

And Pete was quick. He snagged the dog's collar and handed him over to the nearest miner before helping lower the injured guy to the ground. 'Doc...'

All Josh wanted to do was go to Bugsy, figure out how he'd done what he'd done and, more importantly, figure out if he could do more, but his attention had to be on the men.

Caroline, one of the island nurses, was with him, and judging by the fleeting embrace he'd witnessed between them, she was involved with Keanu. She had scissors out already, even as Pete was lowering Reuben to the ground.

Please, let him not need me.

It was silent prayer as he started work. Another compromised blood supply or similar would take all his attention.

But this leg was good. This leg was great.

Or...actually not. It'd hurt like the devil for a week or more but it wasn't broken. It needed careful cleaning, debridement, but it wasn't urgent.

The urgent stuff had been dealt with. And Keanu was here.

'You'll be okay,' he told Rueben. He glanced at Caroline, then at Bugsy, then back to Reuben again. 'We'll give you something for the pain and get you to the hospital but this looks like bruising and lacerations, not a break.'

And then he looked at Bugsy again.

'Do you think Bugsy could find Maddie?' Caroline whispered. He and Caroline were still kneeling over Reuben, but Caroline was following his gaze. 'He's Maddie's dog...'

He wasn't the only one thinking it, then. He glanced at Caroline and saw her fear.

'You're her friend?'

'Yes, not only am I her friend but I'm a Lockhart. My

uncle was supposed to be taking care of this mine and these workers. He clearly failed at that. He's gone and now Maddie's in danger. This is partly my fault. I ordered the closure of the mine but I should have seen that the workers would be in desperate need. I just can't believe that Maddie went in there…'

She looked sick. This was bad for the outside rescue workers, he thought. How much worse would it be for those who'd lived and worked every day with those trapped underground?

And as if on cue, Caroline's phone rang. She flicked it open.

'Maddie. Oh, my God, Maddie, are you okay?' She cast Josh an uncertain look and then flipped the switch to speaker so he could hear. But all he heard was silence.

'Maddie, you've rung the duty phone,' Caroline said urgently into the silence. 'This is Caro.'

'I wanted…' Maddie's voice faltered. 'Caro, I wanted Hettie. I forgot you'd have the phone. Can I…? I need…' Her voice broke on a gasp.

It was too much for Josh. He took the phone from Caroline's hand and spoke.

'Maddie, what's wrong? We can get Hettie to ring you but it might take a few minutes. You sound distressed. Can you tell us what's happening?'

There was another gasp from the end of the line. Pain. Maddie was hurting, he thought. Worse. Maddie was terrified.

'Maddie…'

'I need Hettie,' she whispered. 'I need…'

'Hettie's doing the communication for transport. She's based at the hospital. We'll have her ring you as soon as we can, but you need to tell us why you're hurting.'

Silence seemed to stretch forever, or maybe it was the

fact that Josh wasn't breathing. The whole world seemed to be still. And finally Maddie answered.

'Hettie's the island midwife,' she whispered. 'I need… I need someone to talk me through this. My baby's coming. I think I'm in established labour.'

There were noises around them. Keanu was giving orders in the background. A truck was backing up, ready to transport patients. Beth was talking to someone on the phone.

All Josh could hear was white noise.

Established labour.

There was more silence. He could hear Maddie gasping through the phone. Breathing through a contraction? He knew she couldn't talk.

'How pregnant?' he demanded of Caroline, and it physically hurt to say the words. It physically hurt to wait for the answer.

'She says thirty-four weeks,' Caroline whispered, sounding terrified herself. 'But I suspect… She needs the money to support her mother in that gorgeous nursing home. I know she wants to work for as long as possible. She's due to finish here at the end of this week but I looked at her yesterday and thought the baby's dropped. There's a chance she's a couple of weeks further on.'

Thirty-four weeks. Maybe thirty-six.

Who's the father? But he didn't say it. He hardly even thought it.

Maddie. Underground. In labour.

Thirty-four weeks. A premature baby?

'Maddie,' he said, more urgently, but there was still no answer.

He thought suddenly, searingly, of Maddie five years ago. Maddie lying in the labour ward, holding her tiny son. Mikey had been born impossibly early, never viable from the moment they'd recognised placental insufficiency. But the grief...

Maddie had held their son—*their son*.

He'd walked away. He'd been unable to share his grief and he hadn't been able to help her.

'Maddie?' And this time she answered.

'Y-yes?'

'How far apart are the contractions?' Somehow he kept his voice calm. He was desperately trying to sound like a doctor, when all he wanted to do was to drop the phone and start heaving rocks from the collapsed shaft.

'T-ten minutes. Maybe a bit less.'

'Thirty-four or thirty-six weeks, Maddie? Honest.'

'Thirty-six.'

He breathed out a little at that. It made a difference. For a prem baby, underground, with no medical technology at all, two weeks could make all the difference in the world.

'Malu,' he managed. 'The guy down there with you. Is he your partner?'

There was an audible gasp, and then, unbelievably, he heard the trace of a smile in her voice. 'No. Malu's married to my friend. He has two kids.'

'Can he help you?'

'No.' The sliver of humour disappeared as fast as it had come. 'I need...I need to talk to Hettie. She'll talk me through—'

'I'll put you back to Caroline,' he said in a voice he knew sounded strangled. 'She'll try and organise a line to Hettie. Hold on, love, and—'

'I'm not your love.' It was said with asperity.

'No.' He took a deep breath and somehow steadied himself. Asperity was good, he thought. Asperity meant she still had spirit, strength, the grit he knew and loved. 'The important thing is not to panic,' he told her, but he was all for panicking himself. There wasn't a shred of him that wasn't panicking. 'Hold on, Maddie. We need to do some fast organising.'

He handed the phone back to Caroline.

'Keanu,' he managed in a voice he hardly recognised as his own.

'Yeah?' Keanu was with him in an instant, thinking from Josh's voice it was something urgent, something medical.

It was.

'I want refills of morphine, saline, electrolytes,' he snapped, grabbing his bag then reaching for Keanu's and helping himself. There was a coil of thin rope lying nearby. He slung it over his shoulder. How much stuff could you cart down a collapsing mine? Not enough, but maybe enough to make a difference. 'Can you take over here?'

'What the—?'

'I'm heading down,' he snapped.

'You're going nowhere.' Keanu's hand landed on his shoulder. 'No one goes down that mine.'

'Bugsy's been down and come back again,' Josh snapped, reaching for one of the massive torches one of the miners had set aside. 'If he can, so can I.'

'Bugsy's a dog.'

'Yeah, he's a dog. He has no dependants and he's expendable if necessary. Mate, that's what I am. No one's waiting for me at home and I might make a difference. We have a pregnant woman in labour, an injured miner and the possibility that I might be able to reach them. I'm not trying to dig like the other idiots did. I'm following the path Bugsy's already found. I'm fit and I'm used to tight places. I'm asking no one to come in and rescue me—the responsibility's mine.'

'There's no way.' Keanu growled. 'I can't allow it.'

'You don't have a choice. As I don't. This is my wife.' And suddenly that's exactly what it felt like. He'd walked away from their marriage vows five years ago but she still felt...

Like part of him.

He wasn't married, he thought grimly as he sealed his bag. He didn't do marriage. He hadn't been able to help Maddie in her grief when he'd been unable to handle his own, and it'd almost killed him.

'Pete says the mining engineers are due here in the next half-hour,' Keanu said, urgently. 'They'll assess the risk.'

And he knew exactly what they'd say. They'd seal it. They'd work in inch by painstaking inch. They'd take days to reach her.

Reach *them*.

They'd have the manpower and the authority to stop him. Keanu did, too, if he gave him time to call Pete, to block the mouth by force, to muster all the sensible reasons why he shouldn't try.

'Sorry, mate.' He grabbed a discarded hard hat with attached head lamp and shoved it on his head. 'But this is my wife, my call. Clean things up here. Reuben, I'm leaving you in the best of hands. Oh, and if my boss calls, tell him I'm on family leave. Starting now.'

And then, before Keanu could respond, before another argument could be mounted, he grabbed Bugsy's collar from the miner who was holding him.

'Come on, Bugsy,' he told him, looping the collar hard under his hand. Bugsy had obviously figured the direction to go. He'd gone straight to the injured miners, and then, reluctantly, it seemed, accompanied them to safety.

'Come on, Bugsy,' he told the dog again, and he was at the mine mouth, heading in before anyone could move fast enough to stop him.

CHAPTER FOUR

'MADDIE?'

She'd had to disconnect from Caroline to try and reach Hettie but it hadn't worked. Hettie was manning the phone at the hospital and the line was continuously engaged. She grabbed the phone now, hoping it was Hettie, or, weirdly, hoping even more it was Josh.

That's crazy, she told herself. Just be grateful that you get reception down here, that you have any connection at all.

It wasn't Josh.

'Keanu?'

'Caroline's trying to get a message to Hettie to clear the line so you can talk to her,' he told her. 'Meanwhile, progress?'

'Things are stable. Nothing's changed.' She'd kill for a drink. The contractions were still steady at ten minutes. She ached. Malu was drifting in and out of his drug-induced sleep.

Yes, things were stable.

'Blood pressure?'

'Mine or Malu's?' It was an attempt at humour but it didn't work.

'Both,' he snapped, and listened as she told him.

'That's sounding okay.' But there was serious tension in

Keanu's voice—deep tension—tension that told her something else was going on.

'You're about to tell me the sky's going to fall on our heads? If so, it already has.' She caught herself then and directed her beam upwards. 'Actually, no. No, it hasn't. Bad idea.'

'Can you see any light at all?'

'Um…no.'

'We were hoping you'd be near a ventilation shaft.'

'In which case we'd see light.'

'Not if it's blocked. No.'

'So…' There was still something he wasn't telling her. 'Anything else I can help you with?' She tried to make her voice chirpy, sales assistant like.

'You said you were feeling air.'

Another contraction. She gasped and forgot the sales assistant act. Keanu just had to wait.

'There is the faint whiff of air,' she admitted as she surfaced again.

'It's blowing hard out here, straight into the mouth of the cave. You have the torch? Can you shine it at the rocks, look for gaps?'

She shone. The torch beam simply disappeared into the dust and blackness.

'I can't see anything. Even if there was a way out, I could hardly wiggle. And not with Malu…'

'So if we got someone in to you…'

'No one's to come in.' She must have sounded shrill because Keanu didn't answer for a moment and when he did he sounded deeply concerned.

'Maddie?'

'It's just there's still stuff…settling,' she told him. 'Can't you dig us out from the top?'

'We're working on it. Maddie, you sound like you're in pain.'

'I'm not. I'm worrying. Keanu, no one else is to risk…' And then she stopped. She knew Keanu well. 'Someone's already trying, aren't they? Of all the… There's no room in here. Drill a hole down. Get us out from the top. We can't drag Malu out. There's no room for a stretcher and there are rocks still falling. Burrowing's impossibly perilous. I was an idiot to come in, but I've managed to keep Malu alive. There's no point in me doing that if someone else dies.'

Silence.

'What?' she said, feeling the weight of the silence. 'What aren't you telling me?'

'It's Josh,' he said heavily. 'And Bugsy.'

'What the…?'

'Bugsy went haring into the mine. He found the first two miners, the guys who were helping Malu when you went in. They came out, with him leading. It was almost as if Bugsy knew what he had to do. He got them to the surface but he was heading in again.

'And Josh?' She could scarcely breathe.

'Josh has gone with him. We couldn't stop him. The guy's either a hero or an idiot and I can't decide which.'

'Idiot,' she said, but only half of her meant it.

The other half of her unashamedly wanted Josh.

Torches were almost useless in the dust. The cabled lighting that usually lit the shafts had obviously been knocked out by the fall. The floor was covered with rock litter. Josh wasn't too sure where the roof was, and his torch beam seemed to disappear.

He kept his hand on Bugsy's collar. Bugsy was whining a little, but heading inward and down. He seemed to know exactly where he was going.

If Josh hadn't been holding him he'd have surged ahead. To Maddie?

Who knew? But the fact that he'd found the two miners was an excellent sign. The mine branched out in half a dozen different directions a little way in from the mouth. The miners had been in the tunnel Maddie was in, so he had to assume that was where Bugsy was heading.

To Maddie.

He stumbled on a loose rock and dropped to his knees. Bugsy whined and turned and licked his face, then tugged again.

'You need to go at my pace,' he told the dog. 'Four legs and half my height would be good.'

He tugged. Okay, there was no use sitting around waiting to shrink or grow new legs.

His phone went.

What was it with communications in this place? All the way across the mountains there'd been no signal, yet here…

Maddie. The name popped up on his screen as soon as his fumbling hand hauled his phone from his pocket. He almost dropped it in his haste to answer.

'Hey.' He tried to make his voice normal but the dust was too heavy. He ended up coughing instead.

'You're down the shaft.' Her voice was dull, dread-filled.

'Only a little way down,' he told her. 'Me and Bugsy.'

'Well, turn yourselves around and go back up again.'

'Bugsy won't and I don't know the way without Bugsy.'

'Bugsy took the miners out. They knew enough to say "jeep" and she obeyed. The whole island knows "jeep" to Bugsy means head back to the jeep and stay there. You can't have a dog trailing after you on every island emergency without a few ground rules.'

'So if I say j—' He stopped. 'If I say the name of your car…'

'Say it, Josh.'

'We're coming to find you. Me and Bugsy.'

'You'll kill yourselves and where will that leave us? The engineers will drill in from the top. It's not so deep. They'll find us.'

'It'll take days. Maddie, I'm disconnecting now. Bugsy's eager to keep going.'

'Josh, I don't want this. I didn't expect… You can't risk…'

'You know I always risk. It's what I do.'

'You're trained to swing from helicopters and abseil down cliffs. You're trained in emergency rescue. But for every single scenario you trained and trained. I'm betting not once have you ever trained to dig into a collapsing gold mine when even the experts are saying it's crazy.'

'I'm training now,' he said briefly. 'I'm coming, sweetheart.'

'I don't want you to die!' And it was a wail. She couldn't help herself. Her beautiful Josh…

She loved him. She always had and she always would. He wasn't marriage material. He'd never been her husband, not properly, and years ago she'd stopped hoping for that, and yet she still loved him. The thought of him being down in this appalling place was unbearable.

And then another pain hit. She whimpered before she could stop herself. She bit it off fast, but he'd heard.

'What the…?'

'I just moved on the floor. Sharp rock,' she lied, and heard silence on the end of the line. 'Josh, go home.'

'Conserve your phone batteries, love,' he told her. 'Any minute now you'll get to talk to me in person.'

'I'm not your love,' she repeated.

'Go tell that to someone who cares. I'm coming in anyway.'

He was coming.

She should be appalled. She was appalled.

But…he was coming.

'Help's on its way,' she whispered to Malu, but he was sleeping too deeply to hear.

He needed more fluids. Would Josh be carrying fluids?

'He won't get here.' She said it out loud, trying to suppress the flare of hope, of belief, of trust. 'Okay, Bugsy made it to where the last rockfall took place but there *was* a rockfall.

'It can't be too thick.' She was talking out loud to herself. 'Those guys were with us when it started falling and they ended up safe on the other side.'

She crawled across her little cavern to where the mound of fresh-fallen rock blocked the exit. At least, she thought this was the mound in the direction of the exit. It could be the one behind her.

She was pretty disorientated.

She was in pain.

Forget the pain, she told herself, fiercely now. Concentrate on ways out of here.

Ways Josh could get in.

The rocks were big. The fall wasn't packed with loose gravel, but rather a mound of large boulders.

Dear God, they'd been lucky.

Define luck.

'We have been lucky,' she said out loud. 'If any of these

mothers had hit us we'd have been squashed flatter than
sardines.'

They could still fall. Above her head was a mass of
loose rock, and the shoring timber was cracking.

Don't go there.

Was there a way through the rocks? Was she even looking in the right direction? She played her torch over the
mass. There were gaps in the boulders—of course there
were—but there were more boulders behind. To try and
crawl through...

'He's an idiot to try,' she said out loud. 'Ring him again.'

She knew it'd make no difference.

And for the first time a wash of fear swept over her so
strongly, so fiercely that she felt as if she'd be physically ill.

Josh was out there.

There was nothing she could do. She crawled back to
Malu and put her head next to his on his makeshift pillow.
She pressed her body hard against his. She'd done this be-
fore when he'd needed comfort.

She was doing it again now but it was she who needed
comfort. It was she who needed to escape fear.

'He's coming,' she whispered, and she linked her hands
under her belly and held. Her belly was tight, hard.

Her baby...

'He'll come,' she said, and this time she was talking
to her baby, talking to someone she'd barely been brave
enough to acknowledge as a separate being until now. Was
this why she'd been dumb enough to rush into the mine?
Because she'd hardly had the courage to acknowledge that
this baby could be real?

She'd lost one baby. Mikey's death had left a huge, gap-
ing hole in her life, and it had been a vast act of faith,
a momentous decision, to try again. Once the decision
had been made, she'd gone through the process of find-

ing a sperm donor, the months of hope, the confirmation of pregnancy...

But once that confirmation had come, joy hadn't followed. Terror had followed, that once again she could lose the baby.

She'd coped by blocking it out. She'd not bought any baby clothes. She'd hardly let herself think about it. It was as if by acknowledging she really did have a baby in there she'd jinx it. She couldn't let herself believe that she could hold a little one who might live.

But, belief or not, this baby had rights, too, and one of those rights was not being buried in a collapsing mine before he/she/it was even born.

'I'm sorry,' she whispered as another contraction started to build. 'I'm so sorry I got you into this mess. And I'm even more sorry we're depending on Josh to get us out.'

She was in labour.

The thought was unbelievable. The knowledge was doing his head in.

Somehow he had to put it aside, focussing only on keeping his grip on Bugsy. He was inching ahead, making the big dog slow. Staying safe. He'd be no use to anyone dead. He was taking no unnecessary risks.

In labour.

Who?

Of all the stupid questions? Did he need to know who the father was?

They'd kept in touch. Theirs had been a civilised divorce, born out of grief. Maddie had understood why he couldn't stay married.

She'd said she felt sorry for him.

Why did that slam back now? That last appalling conversation as he'd tossed random stuff into his kit bag, ostensibly heading for a flood in Indonesia. The Australian government had offered help and Cairns Air Sea Rescue had asked for volunteers.

Maybe a month, they'd said.

They'd both known it would be longer. The pain of loss was so great Josh had curled inward inside. He couldn't bear seeing his loss reflected on Maddie's face. He couldn't help her. He couldn't help himself.

'You'll never heal by running away,' Maddie had said sadly, and even then he hadn't been truthful.

'I'm helping others heal. That's why I'm going.'

'You're hiding from the pain the only way you know how,' she'd said. 'But I can't help you, Josh, so maybe it's better this way…'

And then she'd walked out because she couldn't bear to watch him pack, and he was gone before she'd returned.

The end.

Who was the father of her baby? Why hadn't she told him?

This was important.

They got in touch on Christmas and birthdays. Formal stuff.

Babies weren't formal?

New partners weren't important?

He swore.

And then he reached the rock face. The tunnel ended with a mass of fallen boulders and loose gravel.

He raked the floor and saw evidence of the miners who'd been flung apart from Maddie and Malu. A tin canteen. He snagged it and opened it—sandwiches! Worth holding on to? If he could.

If there was anyone to eat them.

He stared at the massive rock pile. It was such a jumble—how could he ever get through?

But Bugsy was nosing forward, whining, clambering up and over the first couple of rocks. He'd let him go—now he made a lunge and grabbed him before he got down the hole he was intent on investigating.

Hole.

Bugsy.

Maddie would never forgive him if he risked her dog.

But contractions… What choice did he have?

He knelt and hugged the big dog close, and he knew what the choice had to be. If this was possible…

Please.

He hauled his coiled rope from his shoulder and tied an end to Bugsy's collar. Then he carefully unrolled the rope so Bugsy felt no pull. It was a light line. It shouldn't cause much friction.

But the chance of a collapse…

Don't think it, he told himself. He couldn't.

He hugged Bugsy one more time, thinking of him all those years ago, thinking of Maddie's joy when he'd put a warm, wriggling bundle of puppy into her arms.

'I'll love him forever,' Maddie had said.

Dared he risk…?

How could he not?

'We're both risking,' he told Bugsy, and he sat back and let the dog go. 'For Maddie.'

And one minute later Bugsy had crawled his way across the first pile of rocks, pushed his nose into a crevice—and then his whole body.

He was gone.

Maddie lay in the dark and worried. A lot.

He could be anyone and I'd be terrified, she told herself. If he was some unknown rescuer putting his life on the line to save her, she'd be appalled.

But, then, no one else would have done it, and she knew it. To head into a mine shaft where the shoring timbers were collapsing, where the shaft was known to be unsafe, where a mass of rock was already blocking the way, was just plain lunacy.

'Idiot hero.' She said it out loud and Malu stirred beside her and she bit her lip.

But still… 'Idiot hero,' she said again under her breath.

But he'd be in his element. She knew that. Josh would do anything for anyone. He was brave, clever, fearless, giving…

But not taking.

If it was Josh stuck in the mine he'd be pulling down more rocks so no one could save him, she told herself, speaking under her breath. Josh being saved? Ha. No one saved Josh.

That was the trouble. When they'd lost Mikey, the giving had been all one way. She'd sobbed and he'd held her but he hadn't wept, as well. He'd held himself close.

And then, when Holly had died, he hadn't even let her hug him. She knew how much he'd loved his little sister, but he'd held himself rigid within his grief and despair, with no way of letting it out.

I don't need help. That was Josh's mantra. How could he live like that?

He did live like that, which was why she couldn't live with him.

I don't need help?

Yeah, if that was the case for her then she should be over at the rock face, reinforcing the rubble so no one could get through. She should be telling Josh that the moment he emerged into her cavern she'd toss rocks at him.

As if.

I don't need help?

She was stuck in a collapsing mine shaft with a guy who was perilously ill. She was in labour. Caroline hadn't been able to put her through to Hettie.

Slowly but surely the contractions were building.

I don't need help?

Some things weren't even worth aiming for.

It was a good thing that Bugsy wasn't a fox terrier. Josh was very, very pleased that the dog was large.

Josh's current plan, albeit a weak one, was to let Bugsy see if he could find a way through the rocks. Bugsy wasn't much smaller than he was across the shoulders. If Bugsy could find a way, then he might be able to follow.

There were, however, a whole lot of unknowns in that equation. And risks.

The best-case scenario was that Bugsy would find a safe passage through, tugging the cord behind him. He'd find Maddie. There'd be a happy reunion. Josh could then follow the rope and get through himself.

The more likely scenario would be that the whole thing was completely blocked and Bugsy would have to back out.

A possible scenario was that Bugsy would become impossibly tangled and stuck.

Or there'd be a further collapse.

Both the final scenarios were unthinkable but beyond the mass of rock was Maddie, and Bugsy seemed as desperate as he was to get through. So there was nothing he could do now but sit and wait and watch the rope feeding out.

There was an initial rush of feed as Bugsy nosed his way past the first few boulders. Then the feed slowed.

And stopped.

Josh's heart almost did the same.

'Bugsy?' he called, but there was no response. And the line started feeding out again.

Was he going straight through? Dear God, had he turned? Could he trap himself?

He could cut the line at this end, as long as the dog didn't get impossibly tangled first.

Whose crazy idea had this been?

The line fed out a little further. And further.

Please...

He'd never pleaded so desperately in his life.

She could hear scrabbling.

It was almost like there were mice in the cave with her, but...scrabbling?

She moved away from Malu's side, almost afraid to breathe in case she was wrong. Then she flicked the torch and searched the rock pile.

She could definitely hear scrabbling and it was getting louder.

It was high up where the rocks almost merged with the ceiling. Or what was left of the ceiling.

If it fell...

She couldn't breathe. She had no room for anything but fear.

Where...where...?

And then there it was, slithering down the face of the cave-in, a great, grey ball of canine dust, a wriggly, ecstatic ball of filthy golden retriever.

And Maddie had the presence of mind—just—to put the torch down before she had an armful of delirious dog, and she was hugging and hugging and pressing her face into Bugsy's filthy coat and bursting into tears.

He was going crazy. Or maybe he already was crazy. There'd been one last, long feed of line, like Bugsy had made a dash—and then nothing. Nothing!

According to the line, the dog didn't appear to be moving. If he'd killed Bugsy...

Of all the stupid, risky, senseless plans. He'd worked for search and rescue for years. There was no way a plan like this could even be considered.

He knew the rules. You played it by the book. You got in the experts, you did careful risk assessment, you weighed up your options. You never, ever put people's lives on the line.

Or dogs'.

Maybe his bosses would okay dogs, he thought bleakly, but surely not Bugsy.

What was happening? Dear God, what was happening?

And then his phone rang.

'Josh.'

She was crying. He could hear her tears. His heart seemed to simply stop.

'Maddie.'

'I have a dog,' she managed. 'I have a whole armload of dog. He's here. Bugsy's here.'

His heart gave a great lurch and seemed to restart. 'Does he still have a cord attached?'

'I...' There was a moment's pause. 'I'll see. It is dark in here.' She said it almost indignantly and he found himself grinning. His lovely, brave Maddie, who always rebounded. 'Yes. Yes, he does. But Josh, what the—'

'I'm coming through, then,' he said. 'Are you hugging Bugsy?'

'Yes, but—'

'Sandwich hug,' he promised. 'Stat.'

'Josh, don't you dare.' He heard her fear surge. 'We have a line through now. Wait for the experts.'

'How far apart are the contractions?'

'I don't…Josh, no!'

'How far, Maddie?'

'I'm not saying.'

'Then you don't need to say. I'm coming in.'

CHAPTER FIVE

JOSH WASN'T A DOG. Dogs were smaller than Josh and they bent more. He was carrying a backpack, necessary if he was to be useful in there, but it made things harder. After a while he tugged it off his back, looped the straps round his ankles and towed it. It was better but still hard.

The fallen rocks were large and angular. Where were smooth river rocks when you needed them? These seemed to have broken with almost slate-like edges, flat and sharp, fine if you walked over a nicely laid path of them but murder to crawl up and around.

But Bugsy had made it through and he would, too. He just had to be careful. Ultra careful. He was following Bugsy's cord, using the head lamp to see, but he was feeling his way, as well. He was testing every rock before he touched it, feeling the rocks above him, trying to take the fewest risks possible. Hauling his pack behind him with his feet. Halting whenever it snagged.

It was so dark. And sharp. And hard.

It was also really, really claustrophobic. He didn't get claustrophobia, he told himself, but another part of him was saying that in this situation claustrophobia was just plain sensible.

At the other end of the cord lay Maddie. Maddie, who was in labour.

He had to be so careful not to pull on the cord so it didn't become dislodged. He was feeding out another line behind him with the idea of ultimate rescue. These cords were lifelines. Meanwhile he was keeping his hard hat on, getting his body through the next crevice, figuring how Bugsy could possibly have got through. Every fibre of his body was tuned to survival.

Bugsy had done it in fifteen minutes. After half an hour Josh was still struggling…

How long could she bear it?

She wanted to ring him but how could she? How could Josh do what he was doing and calmly take time out to answer the phone? He couldn't. She wanted every ounce of his concentration focussed on keeping him safe.

She wanted him out of there.

And she could hear him. That was the worst part. For the last twenty minutes she'd been hearing him hauling his way through the rock. She could hear the occasional shift of earth, the silence as he waited for things to settle. Once she heard the echo of a muffled oath.

She sat and hugged Bugsy. Bugsy whined a little, tugging forward as if he'd go to him—after five years did Bugsy still feel loyalty?—but Maddie was holding tight.

Josh was trying—against all odds—against all sense—to haul himself through impossibly tight, impossibly dangerous conditions. Bugsy had been truly heroic but the last thing Josh needed now was a golden retriever in there with him, licking his face, blocking his way.

She was saying silent prayers, over and over. *Please, let him be safe. Please…*

She'd be saying them for anyone, but for Josh…

She couldn't even begin to understand what she was feeling.

He was her husband.

He wasn't her husband. He was…an old friend?

Liar.

She was no longer curled up by Malu. There was no way she could disguise the contractions now; they were so strong if she lay beside him he'd feel them.

Some doctor she was!

Malu was restless and she knew the pain would break through again soon, leaving him wide awake.

How could she ask a man with such injuries to help deliver a baby?

How could she deliver herself? To put her baby at such risk? This little one who she'd longed for with all her heart and yet hadn't had the courage to acknowledge might be real. This baby who had every right to live.

Could she depend on Josh manoeuvring through these last few yards? Could she dare hope?

Another contraction gripped and she stopped asking stupid questions. Only the one word remained.

Please…

This…had been…a really, really, really…dumb idea. He'd be trapped in here forever, a skeleton, hanging by his fingernails to a stupid rock that, if he could only find purchase, he could use to drag himself up and over.

Bugsy had done it but Bugsy had more toenails than he did. Bugsy's back half wasn't nearly as heavy. She hadn't been hauling a backpack. This thing was imp—

No. He had it. He hauled and felt himself lift.

The cord now seemed like it was running downwards.

Please… It was a silent prayer said over and over. Let this be the last part. Let it open up.

Let me see Maddie.

He gave one last heave, up and over—and suddenly he

was slithering, head first, downwards. He hadn't realised it was so steep. He almost fell, sliding fast on loose shale, the backpack slithering after him.

And then suddenly his head and then his torso were free from the tunnel. He saw light that didn't come from his head lamp.

Torchlight swung towards him, almost blinding him.

'J-Josh?'

And suddenly he was clear. He was on the floor of a cramped cavern that was still a tunnel but after what he'd been in seemed as wide as a house.

But he wasn't noticing. Nothing mattered except that he'd made it and he was holding Maddie in his arms. Holding and holding and holding.

Maddie. His woman.

She'd always felt like that. She'd always been that, from the moment they'd first met, but how much more so in this moment?

He could feel her heart beating against his. She was breathing almost as heavily as he was. He was hugging her and she was hugging right back, maybe even crying.

He wasn't crying. Crying wasn't his style, but holding was.

Why had he let this woman go?

It didn't matter now. Nothing mattered except that she was in his arms, she was safe and they were together.

'Maddie...'

He would have tilted her face. He would have kissed her.

But then there was the slight hiccup of the dog.

Bugsy wasn't letting interpersonal relations get in the way of his needs. He'd orchestrated this rescue and being left out now wasn't going to happen. The dog was wedging his way firmly in between both of them, turning a hug into a sandwich squeeze.

And then, from behind them, a voice.

'Have we got company? I wouldn't mind a hug myself.'

Malu. He put Maddie away from him, just a little, still holding her but loosely so he could see the man lying on the floor.

'Hey, how's the patient?'

'So who's the patient?' Malu managed. 'My Pearl's had two babies, with me beside her every step of the way, so I pretty much know my current treating doctor is well into labour. And her newly arrived backup seems to be one filthy doctor who looks—to my untrained eye, I'll admit—to be bleeding. You'd best fix him up, Maddie,' he told her. 'And then he can fix both of us up next.'

Malu was right. The first priority was actually him. The rocks had been hard and sharp. He'd sliced his arm on that last uncontrolled descent. It wasn't serious but it was bleeding hard and the last thing any of them needed was to lose fluids.

So he tolerated—barely—sitting back while Maddie put pressure on it until the bleeding subsided. She cleaned the cut, pulled it together with Steri-Strips and slapped on a dressing. He made a fast call to Keanu while she did it.

'I'm in.'

Keanu wasted no words. 'Is there a safe way to get them out?'

'No.' He thought about the way he'd had to clamber though. There was a good chance he couldn't get out himself.

If Maddie hadn't been here, maybe he wouldn't have made it. That tunnel was practically suicidal.

But he was here, with Maddie, who was calmly dressing his arm. Between contractions.

'We'll depend on the engineering boys to get us out,' he

told Keanu. 'Short of another collapse, we're safe enough for now. But, sorry, mate, I have work to do. I'll ring as soon as I have things under control.'

Under control? That was a joke.

'It's not my neatest work,' Maddie said, a bit breathlessly, as she finished. 'But you'll do.'

She was breathless and her breathlessness didn't come purely from the dust. 'When was your last contraction?'

'Over ten minutes ago. I'm slowing down. Stress, do you think?'

'So you really are in labour?' Malu's speech was easier now, his body language showing how much it meant to him that someone had been able to get through. 'You didn't admit—'

'There wasn't a lot to admit,' Maddie said with asperity. 'You're not moving and there's no way we can boil water and switch on humidicribs.'

'So you're thirty-six weeks?' They were sitting on the ground. Josh had his arm cradled in front of him. The more he rested it now the less likely it would be to bleed again if...*when* he got busy. 'Tell me why you're still on Wildfire?'

'I'm due to leave on Friday.'

'You know the rules for fly in, fly outs. Thirty-four weeks and then only under strict conditions.'

'I wanted every day of my family leave to be spent with my baby. Leaving six weeks before was a waste of time.'

'Says the woman stuck underground in labour.'

'I didn't intend to get stuck underground,' Maddie said—and sniffed.

The sniff echoed.

'You make our Maddie cry, injured or not, I'll get up and shove you back in that tunnel,' Malu warned. 'And I'll shove a rock back in after you.' He hesitated and his voice faltered a little. 'I don't suppose…Maddie, you can't get out that tunnel hero-boy just came in through.'

'No.' Josh and Maddie spoke together. Maddie, because the thought of crawling through rocks with the massive bulge she had underneath her was unthinkable. Josh…well, pretty much the same for Josh. He'd been incredibly lucky to get here, he conceded. He could well have got himself stuck at any number of places on the way.

'They'll dig down from the top,' he said with more confidence than he felt. He crawled across and lifted Malu's wrist. 'Pain… Scale of one to ten.'

'I'm okay.'

'Answer the question.'

'Seven,' Malu said, reluctantly. 'But I can cope.'

'Forget coping. I have drugs.'

'Maddie has drugs.'

'I have more drugs. Nice drugs.'

'I'd give more for a mouthful of water.'

'I can do that, too. I have a backpack, fully loaded.' He helped the man drink, holding him up a little and then easing him back on his makeshift pillow. Noting the fierce effort it took him not to cry out.

He was in pain, Josh thought, but not from his leg. Ribs?

His breathing was a bit scratchy.

Fractured ribs? Pierced lung?

There weren't a lot of X-ray facilities down there.

'How long since you gave the last morphine?' he asked Maddie.

'I… Half an hour ago. Five milligrams.'

He cast a quick look back at her. She sounded strained.

She was strained. She was leaning against the rock wall, her arms were holding her belly, she was arched back and she was trying not to scream.

He flicked the torch away from her fast, so Malu couldn't see.

Triage. He'd like to do a very fast pelvic examination but Malu was breathing too fast. The pain would be making his breathing rapid and his heart rate rise.

The priority was Malu, but Malu got the world's fastest injection. He set up another bag of saline. Then he hesitated.

'Go to her,' Malu whispered. 'I'm imagining a nice cubicle partition in my mind. I'll close my eyes. Those drugs you gave me…they'll make me sleep, right?'

'They will, but not for ten or fifteen minutes.'

'Tell you what,' Malu said. 'Those empty saline bags… Prop 'em up against the side of my face. Then tell Doc she has all the privacy she could ever want to get that baby out.'

'She's not… It can't be soon.'

'You're the doc and I'm the miner,' Malu whispered. 'But, hell, Doc, I'd go take a look if I were you.'

'I can't have my baby down here.'

That was pretty much what Josh was thinking. He had nothing. Nothing!

Well, that wasn't exactly true. He had basic sterile equipment.

Forceps, not so much. Equipment for an emergency Caesar? Not in his wildest dreams.

'Sweetheart—'

'I'm not your sweetheart.'

'Sorry,' he said, chastened. 'Maddie, I need to examine you.'

'I know you need to examine,' she moaned. 'And I heard what Malu said. Malu, thank you for the privacy but if a vacuum cleaner salesman could stop this pain right now I'd say go ahead, look all you like.'

Malu gave a dozy chuckle.

'Lie back,' Josh told her.

She lay back. He desperately wanted a decent bed. He was asking her to lie on rocks.

He could tug off his shirt to use as a pillow but he was already thinking ahead. If...*when* this baby came he needed something to wrap it in, and things to wrap it in were few and far between.

'So where's your layette?' he demanded, striving for lightness.

'Layette?'

'One of the mums we brought down from Weipa to Cairns last month had a suitcase with her she explained had a full layette. Her mum had knitted it for her. All white. Matinee jackets, bootees, christening robe, tiny wool dresses with pink roses embroidered on them. She went on to have a boy but at least she was prepared.'

'To live in Weipa?' She was gasping, trying to breathe as she obviously knew how to breathe when things got hard. 'With the red dust up there, everything will be pink at first wash.'

'So you don't have a layette.'

'Not here.'

'In Cairns?'

'Not...not even in Cairns,' she admitted. 'I have four weeks to shop.'

He'd helped her tug off her pants, laying them under her hips. That give her a tiny amount of protection from the rocks but not much. Her bra gave her a modicum of privacy, but there wasn't enough of that, either.

Four weeks...

'You're six centimetres dilated,' he told her. 'How many weeks does that give you in the layette-buying plan?'

'I can't...'

'Okay, don't think about it now. Keep doing the breathing. You know how. And stop fighting.'

'Josh, I can't.'

'You and Malu thought you were going to keep this neat little cave a secret, didn't you?' He shifted so he was against the wall as well, then tugged her across him. She protested, but not too much—she was pretty much past protesting. She leaned back against him instead of the wall. He was holding her and that seemed sort of right. His arm was hurting, but in the scheme of things it was nothing. 'And then along comes Bugsy,' he continued, as if this was a completely normal conversation in a completely normal setting. 'And then Josh arrives—and now it seems someone else is coming, too.'

'Josh, you can't. Your arm. You can't hold me. Oh, my…' Her next words were lost in a silent scream. He felt that scream. He felt the contraction take hold of her. He felt her whole body spasm and he held her because it was the only thing he could do.

The contraction eased. She fell back against him with a gasp and his arms tightened.

'You're doing brilliantly. Has anyone told you lately that you're awesome, Dr Haddon?'

'I have.' It was a slurred interjection from Malu in the shadows, and he felt Maddie smile.

'And Bugsy tells me all the time,' Maddie managed.

And then another contraction hit and he thought, How did that happened? Didn't the texts say the rate increased gradually? That had been all of thirty seconds.

'I'm not pushing yet,' she said through gritted teeth as the contraction passed.

'Good for you. You show 'em. This baby comes on your terms or not at all.'

She even managed a wry chuckle.

'Maddie?'

'Mmm…?'

'Is there a dad out there who'll be frantic?'

There was silence at that. He wasn't sure if the silence meant she didn't want to answer, or she couldn't.

The next contraction rolled by without a word, just more of the silent screaming. This woman had courage. There was no way she'd scream.

Come to think of it, this really was a situation where she might literally scream the roof down. The vibrations of a woman in full labour might even be enough to…

Um…don't go there. Not.

Bugsy was whining a little, obviously sensing Maddie's distress. He was nestled as close to them as he could get. Josh had set one of the torches up, just one, aiming it off centre so it wasn't shining directly at them. They were in shadow.

He was still holding her. This was the strangest feeling…

To hold Maddie.

He'd loved holding Maddie. Holding her had been the only time in his life when he'd felt totally at peace.

But… He'd held her the night their baby had died. Or he'd tried to. He remembered the fierce struggle not to sob himself. Something had clenched inside, some hard knot of despair that he still didn't dare unravel, and the same knot had formed when Holly had died.

He hated it. They were two leaden weights he'd carry forever.

But what was he doing, thinking of the start of his marriage, a marriage that had never worked? Focus on now, he told himself. He had no choice. Maddie needed him.

'Just keep the breathing going,' he told her. 'Deep and even. You know the drill.'

'The drill's different when it's me,' she gasped.

'Breathe, sweetheart.'

'Don't call me sweetheart! Just get me out of here.'

He almost smiled. He'd heard that line before, from so many women in labour. *Take me home.*

Where was home?

He and Maddie used to have...

Don't go there, either.

'There's no father,' she muttered through clenched teeth. 'Or at least no one to slug right now. If it was you I'd be knocking your teeth out the back of your head.'

'Hey, it's not the guy's fault.'

'Who else's fault is it? I want someone I can sue.' She was beyond reason now, he thought, caught in pain and trying to find any way through it. 'Hold me tighter,' she demanded. 'Ohhh...'

He held her tighter. Her fingers clenched on his fore-arms. It was just as well it was his upper arm he'd injured. He'd have marks from her fingernails, he thought. Maybe she'd even draw blood.

But donating his arms seemed the least he could do. He so wanted to be needed.

If you don't need me then I don't need you. She'd thrown that at him that last appalling week. *You give and give and give, and you never take, not one inch. And what you give...it's all surface stuff, Josh. You hold yourself so tight, like you're in armour, and I can't get in. I don't want to be the taker forever. I can't be. You need to go.*

And he had. He'd walked away because he'd known she was right.

He couldn't let her in. He couldn't let anyone near the pain he was feeling.

'It was a test tube,' she muttered now. Her whole body

was straining, and the fingers were digging even tighter. 'A vial. Tall, black hair like yours, athletic build, smart, a university student doing his good deed for humanity— for me—by donating semen… What was he thinking? Oooh…'

And she tucked her chin down into her throat and pushed.

'Hey.'

He wanted nothing so much as to stay where he was, holding her. Someone had to hold her, but it could no longer be him.

He was needed at the other end. Someone had to catch.

He needed lights.

He had two torches, one head lamp and Maddie's phone app. He set them all up but still there wasn't enough.

It'd have to do.

He wanted towels. He wanted clean.

He ripped his shirt off but laid it aside. It was thick, serviceable cotton. It was filthy but it was the best he could do. But for a newborn baby with a freshly cut umbilical cord to be wrapped in such a thing…

'I used…I used my shirt for Malu…' Maddie gasped, and he gripped her hand and held.

'That's why I came. To bring you mine.'

'You always did…like an excuse to show your six pack…'

'There are a lot of people to admire it down here,' he told her, and then she moaned and pushed again and he had to deal with what he had: a woman lying in dirt he couldn't protect her from.

The head was crowning. A tiny dark head had emerged at the last push, then gone back as the contraction had eased.

He'd grabbed lubricant from his bag, and gloves. And checked.

The cord... The cord!

'Maddie, I need you to back off.' He tried to make his voice normal, matter-of-fact. 'If you push any harder you'll tear.'

'I need...I need...'

'You don't need to push. Breathe through it, Maddie, and don't push. Don't!'

And she got it. She was a doctor. She knew.

'The cord...'

'It's fine. I just need a little space down here to get things organised. You have to breathe. Hold it, Maddie. Hold.'

And once again that little word was front and centre. Please...

The next contraction hit and he could feel the massive effort it took for Maddie to hold back. To somehow control her body.

The courage of this woman... He had to match it.

One dead baby... There would not be another, he swore. Please.

He had to wait until the contraction eased and it almost killed him.

'H-hurry,' Maddie muttered, and then she swore. 'Hurry, damn you.'

'Do you mind?' he said. 'There are patients present.'

'I'll swear, too, if it helps,' Malu muttered from the shadows, and Josh knew the big miner was feeling as helpless as he was.

Please.

The head had retreated. He had so little time. Where...?

There. He had it. Careful, careful, there was no way he was ripping it...

Hold that contraction.

Now! And somehow it came, slipping seamlessly up and over. The cord was clear and he felt like shouting.

Somehow he made his voice muted but the triumph was there. 'Houston, we have lift-off,' he said in a voice he couldn't possibly hold steady. 'Maddie, the cord's free. Next contraction, go for it.'

And she did. The contraction hit and, risk or not, fear of vibrations or not, there was no way Maddie could keep it in. She hugged her knees and she screamed, a long, primeval scream that echoed and echoed and echoed.

And ten seconds later a tiny, perfect little girl slipped out into that strange new world.

'You have a daughter,' Josh managed, and he couldn't stop himself. He was staring down at the slip of a baby in his hands and tears were streaming unchecked down his face.

'Let me…let me…'

What was he thinking? Every textbook in the land said bring the baby straight up to the mother, place the baby on the mother's breast while you cope with the umbilical cord, even let the mother discover the baby's sex for herself.

He slid the tiny scrap of newborn humanity up to her mother. Maddie's arms enfolded her.

Josh laid his shirt over the top of both of them—he wanted no dust or scraps of rock falling on this little one. He'd cope with the umbilical cord soon. It was good to leave it for a minute or two to stop pulsing, he told himself. And besides…

Besides, there was no way he was cutting anything through tears.

'A daughter.' It was Malu, whispering again from the shadows. 'Hey, a little girl. Congratulations to you both.'

And that was what it felt like, Josh thought. *Both.*

This little girl was nothing to do with him. She was the daughter of his ex-wife and an unknown donor. She had no biological connection to him at all.

But he glanced down at the woman cradling her newborn in her arms, at the look of unimaginable awe on Maddie's face, and he knew…

Biological connection or not, he'd defend this little family to the death.

There were so many emotions coursing through Maddie's mind that she had no hope of sorting them.

She was beyond trying. Josh had laid her tiny daughter on her breast. She was lying on her mother's naked skin, a tiny scrap of humanity.

Her daughter.

Josh had settled his shirt over the pair of them, but under the shirt she was cradling her daughter. Her hands enfolded her, feeling the warmth, the wetness, the miracle.

The tiny girl hadn't cried but she was making tiny, waffling grunts, as if she wasn't the least bit scared but rather she was awed at the amazing world she'd emerged into.

Her daughter.

She'd had the cord around her neck…

The tiny part of Maddie that was still a doctor let that thought drift.

If Josh hadn't been here…

He was. Her Josh, riding to the rescue.

It was what he was good at. It was what she most loved—and hated—about him.

But for now she was no longer capable of processing the whys and the wherefores. Too much emotion, too much pain, and now…too much wonder?

'She's snuffling,' Josh said, and she could hear him smiling. 'I can guess what she's looking for.'

'My bra... It unclips at the front...'

'Great forethought,' he said, but he had to use the torch again to help her unclip it, and he smiled and smiled as her baby girl figured exactly what was going on. He stroked the tiny face, she turned in the direction of his stroking finger, found what he was directing her to...and made her connection.

Maddie gasped and gasped again. How could this be happening? Something so wonderful?

She had a daughter.

A memory flashed back, or maybe not a memory. It was the bone-deep truth that she'd held Mikey like this. That she'd loved her son.

She glanced up and she saw in Josh's face that he knew it, too. It was a bittersweet moment, but strangely it didn't hurt.

And it was good that Josh was here to share it with her, she thought. Josh had never admitted how much Mikey's loss had hurt him, but she knew it had, and somehow, right now, it was important that he was here. Whether he'd admit it or not, this was a joy to be shared, but it was also the remembrance of sorrow. Somehow, Mikey was with them. Somehow, right now, she felt...married?

'Th-thank you for being here,' she whispered to Josh. 'Oh, Josh.'

'Hey,' he said softly into the shadows, and he touched her cheek, a feather touch, a caress, a gesture of love and admiration and...awe?

And then, because he couldn't help himself, or maybe it was her doing, maybe she'd turned her face to him, maybe because it seemed right, inevitable, an extension of this whole amazing moment... For whatever reason, he bent and placed his lips on hers. He kissed her.

* * *

'Josh?'

The phone was ringing. Maybe it'd been ringing for a while. No one had noticed and he didn't want to notice now.

The kiss was magic. The kiss was like putting back a part of his body he hadn't known had been removed. The kiss was…right.

But Maddie was stiffening a little and she'd managed to get his name out. She was right. The kiss had to end.

Obstetrician kissing mother?

He hadn't felt the least bit like an obstetrician. There were no foundations for how he'd felt, but still… For a few amazing moments he'd felt like a man in love with his wife. Remembering his son. Welcoming his daughter.

But that wasn't reality. Reality was that the kiss was over. Reality was that he was stuck underground in a mine. He was officially part of the rescue team and making contact had to be the first priority.

He was here to work.

Still, he'd missed the call and Keanu had to ring again, and by the time he answered, Keanu's first word was a shout.

'Josh!'

'I'm here, mate. There's no need to burst my eardrum.'

'What the hell's going on? We heard a scream. Hell, Josh.'

It had been quite a scream. It must have echoed up and out through the shafts.

If he'd been out there he'd have been going out of his mind.

He wasn't. He was in here.

All was quiet in the confines of the tiny cavern. He had a sudden, almost unbearable urge to cut the connection and keep the world at bay.

There was a dumb thought.

'What's happened?' Keanu was demanding. 'Another cave-in? Why haven't you been answering?'

Had the phone been ringing for a while, then? 'We've been busy.'

'The tunnel. Is it safe for me to come in?'

'No.' He knew that absolutely. He'd had amazing luck to get through himself.

'Hell, Josh. We're going out of our minds out here. Why didn't you answer?'

'Triage. We had a bit of a medical emergency but it's okay.'

'Medical emergency?' Keanu's voice was sharp with worry. 'It was a woman's scream. Was it Maddie? Is she hurt? What's going on?'

'Women's business,' he said, and he allowed himself a smile. 'We're on the other side of it now.'

'Women's business…'

'Yeah, and, Keanu…you know you were thinking there'd be three people and a dog to dig out?'

'Yeah?' Keanu sounded dazed.

'Make it four. We have a new arrival. Mother and daughter are doing fine. Malu and I could use cigars but if cigars aren't forthcoming a ruddy great bulldozer with a bit of finesse will do fine.'

CHAPTER SIX

A RUDDY GREAT bulldozer took time to organise. The experts had now arrived from the mainland. There'd be no more heroics. Things were being done by the book.

But because of Josh's forethought there was a further link to aboveground.

Josh had attached a cord to Bugsy when he'd sent the dog to find his mistress. When he'd come in himself, he'd hauled in another behind him. That meant they had two cords running through the caved-in rocks, cords that could be linked, like a raft fording a river. One cord got pulled in, with something attached. The attached thing was removed, the other cord was used to pull it back out. Back and forth. Josh had used the system in tight spots before, though never for himself.

Their team had bags designed for the purpose, tough and slippery. While the team from Cairns started their work aboveground the bags started their cautious way back and forth.

The first bag they tried contained tougher cable. The important thing was not to break the link. Then, with both cords set up as slippery cable rather than nylon, Keanu started sending in supplies.

First came fluids—not much on the first pull, as they didn't want to risk anything getting stuck. But Keanu also risked sending in wipes and a blanket in which to wrap the baby.

Also a diaper.

There was also a card, very makeshift, written on the back of a mine safety notice.

A big welcome to Baby Haddon, the card said. *From all of us on the surface. But isn't the stork supposed to go down chimneys, not mine shafts?*

He read it to Maddie and it made her smile. Or smile more.

'That'll be Hettie,' she said, sounding a bit choked up. 'She's such a friend. I have so many good friends here.'

She had a whole life he knew nothing about, Josh realised as he retied the empty bag to the cord and sent a text for the guys out there to pull.

Then they went back to the waiting game while Keanu organised more stuff to come in.

Malu had finally let the effects of the painkillers take hold and was deeply asleep. Bugsy was also dozing, pressed close to his mistress. The baby had taken her first tentative suckle and drifted to sleep, as well.

Josh flicked the torch off and moved again to sit behind Maddie. She tried to object. 'I don't mind hard...' but he was having none of it. He was her pillow and they were alone in their cocoon of darkness.

It felt right. He was meant to hold her, he thought. His body thought so.

Danger or not, cradling this woman felt wonderful.

'So when did you decide to have a baby?' he asked into the silence, though he had no right to ask such a question and she had every right to refuse to answer.

Silence.

'Sleep if you want,' he murmured, letting her off the hook, but he felt rather than saw her shake her head.

'I don't feel like sleep yet. I know this is an appalling situation but all I can feel is happy. If you knew how much I wanted this…'

'I guess…I did know.'

'But you didn't want it.'

And there was a game-changer. The peace dissipated from the darkness and he let her accusation drift. Had he wanted this? A wife? A baby?

Not enough to take risks. Not enough to risk the pain he'd felt last time.

'I'm sorry,' she whispered. 'That was uncalled for. It's okay, Josh, I'm not about to dredge up the past. The truth is that I reached thirty-four last birthday and I thought if I don't do something soon I'll end up without a family. I know that sounds selfish but there it is. I wanted it so much.'

'Not enough to remarry?' He tried to say it lightly— and failed.

'I hardly have time for marriage.' She was trying for lightness, too, he thought. 'I work here fourteen days straight and then I have a week back in Cairns. I spend most of that time with Mum.'

'Wouldn't it have been better to get a job in Cairns?'

'Maybe.' This was none of his business and he could almost hear her thinking it, but she didn't say it.

'You know, it's really hard to say goodbye,' she said at last, hesitatingly, almost as if she was thinking it through as she spoke. 'The stroke damaged Mum mentally, but she still knows me and she still loves me visiting. But if I only have an hour, she clings and sobs when I leave. If I use a whole day, though… I take her out for walks, I give her meals and I read to her. Finally she goes to sleep happy. The nurses say the next day, when I'm not there, she's peaceful, not distressed. So if I worked in Cairns, I couldn't just pop in and out. It'd be too upsetting for all of us. But this way there are hardly any goodbyes. It's a private nursing home. It costs a bomb but fly in, fly out doctors get paid a bomb. This is the only way I can keep her there, and it works.'

'I told you I'd help!' It was an exclamation of anger, reverberating round the tunnel, and he felt rather than saw her wince.

'I told you, Josh. I'm done needing you.'

'You needed me today.'

'I did,' she said, and shifted a little and cradled her daughter just a wee bit tighter. 'And I'm so grateful.'

'So why won't you let me do more?'

'We've had this out,' she said, wearily now, and he flinched. The last thing he wanted was to make her tired.

'I'm sorry. We can talk about this later.'

'No, we can't. I shouldn't have kissed you.'

'You still…love me.' Why had he said it? But it wasn't a question. It was a statement of fact, and he waited for her to refute it.

She didn't. She was his woman, and he was cradling her with every ounce of love and protection he was capable of.

'Yes, Josh, I still love you,' she said at last, even more wearily. 'And I'm guessing… You're thinking you still love me.'

'I always have.'

'Within limits.'

'Maddie…'

'But loving's not for limits,' she whispered into the darkness, as if she was suddenly sure she was right. 'Look at my beautiful Lea.'

'Lea?'

'After a friend, here on the islands. And Lea Grace for my mum. I can't wait to show her to Mum. I know Mum's damaged but you know what? She'll think the sun rises and sets from her granddaughter. Unconditional love. That's what I'll give my Lea, from now until eternity.'

'I would have loved you…'

'If I let you. You said that. But your love had conditions.'

'It didn't.'

'It did,' she said, steadily and surely. 'As long as love is one-directional it's fine by you. You're allowed to love me all you want. But me…'

'Maddie…'

'No, let me say it,' she whispered. It was weird, sitting in this appalling place, locked in by total blackness. By rights they should still be terrified, but Lea's birth had changed things. This seemed a place of peace. Even Malu's breathing had settled, reassuring them all.

'Josh, when Mikey died it broke your heart.' She said it steadily into the stillness. 'I know it did, but you couldn't show it. You couldn't take comfort.'

'I didn't need to.'

'Yes, you did,' she said, still surely. 'But you were afraid if you showed it you'd break. You comforted me but when I cried you couldn't cry with me. You were my rock but I didn't need a rock. Mikey had two parents. Only one was allowed to grieve.'

'Maddie…'

'And then when Holly died it was worse,' she whispered. 'Because you were the one who was grief-stricken, but how could you let it out? How could you share? I could see the war you were waging but there wasn't a thing I could do to help. You have this armour, and it's so strong there's no way I can get through. And I can't live with armour, Josh. Just…loving…isn't enough.'

He didn't answer. Guilty as charged, he thought, but what could he do about it?

'It's okay,' she said, steadily now, and he wondered how she could sound so strong after what she'd been through. But she was strong, his Maddie.

His Maddie?

She wasn't his Maddie. They'd decided to end their marriage for the most logical of reasons and those reasons still stood.

His arms were around her. She was cradling her tiny new daughter and he knew if anything happened to either of them his heart would break.

But he couldn't share. That way… To open himself to such pain, to let the world see him exposed.

Maddie called it armour and maybe it was.

And, yes, he still needed it.

Out there be dragons.

She was right. He did have armour, and without it he had no weapon fierce enough to face them.

His phone rang. Thank you, he said silently as he answered. Thinking was doing his head in. Thinking while holding Maddie was doing his head in.

Keanu.

'Another bag coming in,' Keanu told him. 'This one has air mattresses and a pump. It's safer if we pull in tandem.'

Which meant moving away from Maddie. She'd heard what Keanu had said and was already shifting slightly so he could move.

He hated leaving her.

But air mattresses… To lie on air rather than solid rock… It was imperative for both Malu and for Maddie.

'I'll miss my Josh cushion,' Maddie said, and he knew she'd said it lightly. But to Josh, right then, it didn't sound light at all.

* * *

Air mattresses. Dust masks. Food packs and drinks.

All the essentials to let them live.

And then Malu decided he might not.

He'd seemed okay. Josh had even let him use the phone to talk to Pearl. Pearl's terror had resounded through the shaft—there was no room for privacy here—but after a couple of moments the calm, gruff voice of her miner husband seemed to have settled the worst of her fears.

'We're looking after him,' Josh had told Pearl before they'd disconnected. 'He has two doctors dancing attendance every moment. He wouldn't get that sort of attention in the best city hospital.'

'Oh, but you have a baby.' Pearl was so weepy.

He had a baby? Not so much.

'Maddie has a daughter, yes,' he told her, and he couldn't help himself, he had to flick on his torch and let light fall on the woman holding her tiny bundle. No woman could look more contented.

You have a baby? No. This was Maddie's baby. They were separate.

Because he was afraid?

This was hardly the time to think about that. 'Are you telling me Dr Maddie can't cope with a newborn and any medical emergency that could possibly arise?' he demanded of Pearl. 'She's a superwoman, your Doc Maddie.'

And there it was again. *Your Doc Maddie.*

Not his.

'I…I know she is.' Pearl faltered.

'But we don't need her,' Josh said firmly. 'Malu's recovering. He'll emerge battered and bruised—we all will. But for now we have air beds, we have plenty of supplies, we have a new baby to admire and we seem safe. Pearl, we're okay.'

Except they weren't.

How late was it—or how early—when Malu's breathing changed?

Josh must have dozed but Maddie touched him and he was wide awake in an instant.

'What do you need?'

'Listen to Malu.'

She would never have woken him if there wasn't a worry. Maddie was a seriously good doctor. He flicked on the torch and was at Malu's side in an instant.

And he heard what Maddie was hearing.

He'd checked Malu before he'd allowed himself to sleep and Malu had been breathing deeply and evenly. The morphine was effective. He had an air mattress and pillow, and a light mask to keep the dust at bay.

Josh had checked him thoroughly, knowing the bruises and pain from his chest signified probable fractured ribs. There had, however, been no sign of internal problems.

There were problems now. Malu's breathing was fast and shallow. He was staring up at the roof, his eyes wide and fearful. As Josh's torch flicked on, he turned and gazed at Josh in terror.

'I can't...I can't...'

Pneumothorax? Haemothorax? The words crashed into Josh's mind with a sickening jolt.

His mind was racing through causes. Probable broken ribs... The ribs had caused no problems until now, but maybe in his relaxed state, with the morphine taking hold and giving Malu's body a false sense of security, the big man had shifted in his sleep.

And a fractured rib had shifted. If indeed the lung was punctured, every time Malu breathed, a little air would escape into the chest wall. And then a little more, and a little more...

There was no open wound. The air couldn't escape. The pressure would finally collapse first one lung and then the other.

Was he right? Almost before he'd thought it, he had Maddie's stethoscope in his ears, listening at the midaxillary line. Normally he'd listen at the back as well, but there was no way he was shifting Malu and risking more damage with those ribs.

Unequal bilateral breath sounds. Diminished on the right.

Very diminished.

If Malu had presented in an emergency room with suspected fractured ribs, he would have been X-rayed straight away, but up until now his breathing had been fine. That was all Josh had had to go on.

'What…what's happening?' Malu gasped, and Josh took a moment to regroup. He needed to move fast, but panicking Malu would speed his breathing even more.

'I reckon you've somehow scraped your lung and made a small tear,' he told him. 'It's not too big or it would have caused problems before this, but if we're to get you breathing comfortably again we need to do something about it.'

'What…?'

Behind him Josh sensed Maddie reaching for the phone. They had two doctors, he thought, and the knowledge was reassuring, even if one was only hours post-baby.

'Keanu? We have a slight problem.' Maddie's voice was calmly efficient, as if a tension pneumothorax was something she saw twice a day before breakfast. 'We need a bag in here, with equipment…'

She knew that they didn't have the right equipment with them. She'd hauled her bag in when she'd run in. He'd brought in a bit more but now they needed specialist gear.

Part of his job was road trauma—actually, any kind of trauma. He had what he needed at ground level, in his emergency bag, the gear he'd packed so carefully back in Cairns.

'Let me speak to Keanu,' he told Maddie, and then he summoned a grin for Malu. 'Maddie's better at the bedside manner than I am. Is Lea asleep? Praise be. Our Maddie's just had the world's fastest maternity leave, and she's ready to move on.' And he held his hand out for the phone.

And Maddie had it figured, exactly what was needed of her right now. She edged forward—gingerly—who wouldn't edge gingerly so few hours after birth? Josh dragged his air bed to Malu's side so she had something soft to settle on.

'Let me tell you what I think's happening inside you,' Maddie said to Malu. 'It's really interesting. But, hey, I want you to even out your breaths while I talk. Nice and slow, nice and slow. I know it feels like you're a fish out of water, but we have time not to panic. Do you know what a pneumothorax is?' And she kept on talking, calm and steady, and Josh thought if he didn't know better he might even feel calm and steady, as well.

She was some doctor.

She was some woman.

But there wasn't time for focussing on Maddie. Keanu was on the end of the line, waiting with almost rigidly imposed patience. Maddie had said there was a problem. He'd know better than to demand details until they were ready to give them.

'Malu's developed a tension pneumothorax or haemothorax,' he said curtly, while Maddie's reassuring tones made a divide between Josh and his patient.

'Tension… Hell, Josh, are you sure?'

'Sure. A slight shift must have caused a leak. Unequal bilateral breathing. Subcutaneous emphysema and tenderness, shortness of breath and chest pain. I'm thinking fractured rib is the only answer. Mate, I need gear in here fast. We need oxygen, plus local anaesthetic and equipment to get it into the intercostal space. I need a chest tube for drainage.'

'Mate—'

'Yeah,' Josh said, cutting him off. He knew exactly what Keanu wanted to say—that operating in conditions like this was unthinkable. How to keep a wound clean, a tube clear? 'But there's no choice. Send down a flutter valve but I'm thinking this place is too messy to rely on that alone. We'll use an underwater seal drain. I haven't used one for years but you'll find a three-chamber unit at the bottom of my kit. Also more saline. A lot more saline. Start getting it in now, drugs first. We have gloves and basic equipment here to keep things almost sterile.'

'Do you have enough light?' Keanu still sounded incredulous.

'Our Maddie will hold the torch while I operate. She's a hero, our Maddie. The lady with the lamp. Florence Nightingale has nothing on our Maddie.'

And Maddie heard. She turned a little and gave him a lopsided grin.

'Did you hear that?' she asked Malu. 'Josh reckons I'm great. Well, I reckon he's great so that's settled. We have two great doctors and one patient with a teeny, tiny tear in his middle. Nothing to this, then. Piece of cake.'

'What else do you need?' Keanu snapped, and Josh could hear the tension in the island doctor's voice. It was all very well playing the hero in the middle of hands-on action, he thought, but standing helplessly at the minehead, knowing there was nothing you could do to help, would be a thousand times harder.

But he needed to concentrate on practicalities. Thinking of others' distress only muddied the waters.

Focus.

'I need a fourteen-gauge angiocath and at least a four-centimetre needle,' he told Keanu, hauling himself back from the brink as he always did in a crisis. If there was urgent need, he had to block everything else out. 'We need anaesthetic, tubing, more antiseptic, more gloves. I need a good clean sheet—when this is done I want Manu and his drainage tube protected from grit. If you can get it in fast, we're good to go.'

'That's all?'

'Plus anything else you can think of,' Josh replied. He wouldn't mind a clearer head to think things through. His arm was throbbing. His own breathing was a bit compromised—the grit was working through the mask and there was still that piercing knowledge of the danger they were in. That Maddie and her baby were in...

Do not go there.

'Actually, a ruddy big hole for lifting everyone out would be great,' he added dryly, and was dumb enough to feel proud he'd kept the emotion from his voice.

'We're working on it,' Keanu told him. 'Is Maddie okay?'

'I'm a whizz,' Maddie said, hearing Keanu's sharp query and taking the phone. She even managed to grin happily down at Malu, as if popping down mine shafts and doing emergency surgery right after childbirth was part of her normal working life. 'I'm practically boring Malu to sleep now, but we might need to up the anaesthetic a bit. Keanu, just tie everything up with pink ribbons as my baby shower and send it right down.'

* * *

'What are their chances?'

In the clearing at the mine mouth the men and women were looking grim.

Caroline had been efficiency plus since she'd arrived at the site, but she'd suddenly broken down. Beth was crouched beside her, hugging her.

In the background things were happening. There could be no bulldozers here. One hint of heavy machinery and the entire shaft could crumble.

The odds were being spelled out to all. Caroline had been washing out grit from a miner's eyes. She'd finished what she'd been doing, calmly reassured the guy she'd worked on—and then walked to the edge of the clearing and sobbed.

Beth had been watching her. Helpless R Us, Beth thought. Usually in a disaster such as this there were things she could do. Work was the best medicine, the best distraction from fear.

Here, though, the work for the medical team had dried up. Keanu was acting as communicator, organising the bags that were being carefully manoeuvred underground.

Caroline and Beth were left with nothing to do.

Except fear.

'We have the best team possible,' Beth told Caroline now. 'The best engineers… We've been on to Max Lockhart—apparently he owns this mine. He, like all of us, assumed it was closed, and he's appalled.'

'He would be,' Caroline whispered. 'He's…he's my father.'

'Your father?'

'He lives in Sydney. My uncle Ian's been in charge here. Dad…Dad has problems.'

'No matter,' Beth said soundly. 'Whatever he is, he's

moving heaven and earth to get resources here. There's a massive mining operation just north of Cairns. He's been on to them. See those guys over there? That's where they come from and this is what they do, deal with mine collapses. They're saying they'll drill side on to the collapsed shaft where the rock's more solid. Then they'll pick their way across to our guys.'

'But it'll take so long... And Maddie...' Once the tears had come, Caroline was no longer able to stop them.

'We have time.' This was what Beth was good at—that and shimmying down rope ladders and hauling people out of overturned cars, but, hey, she had a few skills, and reassurance was in her bundle. 'The bag pulley system seems to be working well.'

'But how can they stay there? Keanu says the blocked area is no longer than ten feet long. A woman who's just given birth...'

'They have food, water, air and light,' Beth said solidly, maybe more solidly than she was feeling. 'We even have little bathroom bags, like they have in spaceships. We pull 'em out every time the pulley comes this way. We can even send in deodorant if it's needed. Not that your Maddie would smell, but Josh and Malu in a tight spot... All that male testosterone... Come to think of it, I will send in some deodorant. Maddie must be just about ready to pass out.'

And Caroline chuckled. It was a watery chuckle but it was a chuckle all the same.

'But this operation...' she whispered. 'With the rock so unstable... You really think they can be okay?'

'We have two skilled doctors underground and the best mine experts on top of the ground,' Beth told her. 'Of course they'll be okay. You'd better believe it.'

And then Keanu came over to talk to them, to hug Caroline, to add his reassurances.

Of course they'll be okay.

You'd better believe it?

'Please, let me believe it, too,' Beth muttered to herself as she moved away. 'Please.'

CHAPTER SEVEN

THEY HAD ALL the gear. Malu was as settled as they could make him. The pneumothorax had to be fixed now.

There was one slight problem.

Josh's right hand shook.

Maddie had cleaned the gash on his arm and pulled it together with Steri-Strips, but it ran almost from his elbow to his shoulder.

He hadn't lost sensation. There was no reason why his hand should shake.

It shook.

Maddie had prepped and draped Malu's underarm. She'd used ketamine as an adjunct to the morphine, making Malu dozy but not soundly asleep.

What was needed now was local anaesthetic. It was a procedure that needed care, knowledge and a steady hand. The anaesthetic needed to be infiltrated through the layers of the chest wall, onto the rib below the intercostal space. The needle then had to be angled above the rib and advanced slowly until air was aspirated. The last five mils of the anaesthetic needed to be injected into the pleural space.

Josh knew exactly what to do. He'd done it before. He'd do it again—this was his job, trauma medicine.

His hand shook.

'Josh?' Maddie's voice was a soft whisper. She was holding the torch.

She'd have seen the tremor.

'I can do this,' he muttered under his breath, and he closed his eyes and counted to ten, trying desperately to steady himself.

He opened his eyes and his hand still shook.

I can't. But he didn't say it. Malu was still sleepily conscious. The last thing Malu needed was to sense indecision in his surgical team. Instead, he glanced up at Maddie, their eyes locked and held…

I can't.

'Slight change of roles,' Maddie said, without so much as a break in her voice. It was like this was totally normal, first cut one toenail, then cut another. 'Malu, Josh is looking at your ribs and thinking you don't need his great masculine forefinger to be making a ruddy big hole. Not when we have my dainty digits at the ready. So we're swapping. Hold on a second, Dr Campbell, while I scrub and glove. It now seems I get to play doctor while Josh plays the lady with the lamp.'

And Malu even smiled.

She was amazing, Josh thought as he took the torch from her. She'd made what was happening sound almost normal. She was stunning.

She was hours after giving birth. How could she?

'Maddie, can you?'

'Steady as a rock,' she said, smiling at him with all the assurance in the world, and she held up her hands to show there wasn't the hint of a tremor. There should have been. After what she'd gone through. 'Though we're hoping Malu's not rocklike. Malu, if you've been working out I might need to get a drill rather than a teeny, tiny needle.

Why you guys think you need muscles is beyond me. Give me a guy with a one pack rather than a six pack any day.'

She was still distracting Malu. He was holding the torch—he could hardly help her on with her gloves but she used the backup method—using one sterile glove to tug on another. It wasted gloves but this wasn't the time to be arguing. Instead…he could do a bit of distracting, too.

'So you'd have loved me better if I'd had a bit of flab?' he demanded.

'The odd sign of humanity never hurt anyone,' she said, turning back to the instruments they'd laid out ready. Dust was still settling. Contaminants were everywhere. There were real risks here, but the alternative was unthinkable. 'I never did have much use for Spider-Man.'

'I guess that's what ended our marriage,' Josh said, managing a grin for Malu. 'Though I would have described myself more as Batman. He was so smooth in his other life.'

'Yeah, six pack in one, smarmy in the other. You ready, Malu? It's going to sting.'

'If he's Batman, I can do the hero bit, too,' Malu managed. 'Do your worst, Doc. Just get this breathing under control.'

He'd thought it would be the hardest thing in the world, to be aboveground, not knowing what was going on.

He was wrong. The hardest thing was doing what he was doing now, which was exactly nothing.

Except holding the torch. If Maddie wasn't totally reliant on the light he was holding maybe he could move behind her, support her a little. What he was demanding of her seemed impossible.

How dared his arm shake?

To have to ask for help… To be dependent on Maddie…

It wasn't him who was dependent on Maddie, he reminded himself. It was Malu. He was under no illusions, Malu's life was under her hands.

But they were steady hands, and there was no doubting their skill. He watched, every nerve attuned to what she was doing, as she carefully, carefully manoeuvred the anaesthetic to where it was needed.

Malu hardly responded as the needle went in. The morphine and ketamine were doing their job—but also, Malu was growing weaker. How much lung capacity did he have left?

To do so much and have him die now...

Stop thinking forward, he told himself. That was the problem with doing nothing—he had time to think.

Josh's work was his lifeline. When things hurt, when emotion threatened to overwhelm him, work was what he did. It stopped the hurt, or at least it pushed it so far onto the back burner that he didn't have to confront it.

They were waiting for the anaesthetic to take hold. Maddie was staring down at the sterile cloth holding her instruments. There was a risk dust would settle on the cleaned tools but there was little they could do about it. Josh was holding the torch with his steady hand. He couldn't do much assisting with the other.

She was practising what she needed to do in her head.

How many times had he watched her skill in a medical setting?

They'd met—how many years ago? He'd been a registrar at Sydney Central's emergency unit. Maddie had been a first-year intern, trying emergency medicine out for size.

She'd been one of the best interns he'd ever met. She'd been calm in a crisis, warm, reassuring and clever.

He'd tried to persuade her to stay, to train in the specialty he loved.

'Emergency medicine's great,' he remembered telling her. 'You live on adrenaline. You save lives. Every time you turn around there's a new challenge.'

'But you never get to know your patients,' she'd said, and she'd said it over and over as his professional persuasion had turned a lot more personal. Soon it hadn't been Dr Campbell trying to persuade Dr Haddon to change career direction, but it had been Josh persuading Maddie to marry him.

'Ready,' she said now, and he shoved the memories away and focussed. Even if his role was minor, the light was still crucial. Her fingers could never be allowed to shadow what she was doing.

But it nearly killed him to watch. What she was doing was so important. He was trained for this. This was his job, whereas Maddie...

This was still part of her job and, unpractised or not, she seemed to know exactly what she was doing. Her fingers were rock steady as she made the incision along the border of the intercostal space. She made it deep and long enough to accommodate her finger.

She glanced up at Josh then, a fast glance that said she wasn't as sure as her actions made out, but then she was focussed again.

'You're doing great,' he told her, but she wasn't listening.

She needed a nurse with swabs. Maybe he could swab, but if the light wobbled...

'In,' she said, and as the tissue was pushed aside by the insertion of her finger he heard the tiny rush of out-coming air.

She had the curved clamp now, using blunt dissection only, using the clamp to spread and split the muscle tissue.

She was in the pleural cavity. She'd be exploring, looking for adhesions. Making lightning-fast assessments.

He wanted to talk her through what was happening, but her face said it all. She was using all her concentration and then some.

'Going great,' he repeated, and then, as Malu flinched, not with pain, he thought, but maybe with tension because breathing was so darned hard, he took the miner's hand with his shaky one and gripped.

They both watched Maddie.

And watching Maddie…

He'd forgotten how much he missed her. He remembered that first time he'd seen her as a newly fledged intern. She'd been comforting a frightened child.

He'd been called to help but he'd paused in the doorway, caught by the sight of her. Something had changed, right at that moment.

Something he'd been denying ever since? That he needed her?

She was putting the chest tube in now, mounting it on the curved clamp and passing it along the pleural cavity. He heard Malu's breath rasp in and rasp in again, like a man who'd been drowning but had just reached the surface. Finally, blessedly, he saw the almost imperceptible shift at Malu's throat. It was imperceptible unless you were looking for it. It was imperceptible unless you knew that the lungs were re-inflating, that what was in the chest cavity was realigning to where it should be.

'Done,' Maddie murmured, and he did hear shakiness now, but it was in her voice, not in her hands. She was still working, but on the exterior, suturing the tube into place. She'd taken a moment to tug off her gloves and put on new ones before she worked on the exterior of the wound. She shouldn't have needed to. If she'd had an assistant…

She didn't. She was working alone.

He could have told her how to operate the underwater seal but he didn't need to. She knew how.

He could have helped her dress the incision area but he didn't need to do that, either.

She was a doctor operating at her best.

She didn't need him.

The words hung. A shadow…

Had he been too afraid to admit he needed her?

The tube was now firmly connected to the underwater seal. He could see the bubbles as air escaped the pleural cavity. The loss of this tiny amount of air wasn't enough to cause Malu major problems. Building up in the pleural cavity, it was lethal. Calmly bubbling out into water, it was harmless.

Job done. The dressing was in place. Maddie sat back on her heels—and he saw the energy drain out of her.

She swayed.

And finally, finally there was something he could do. She did need him. He moved before he even knew he intended moving. He took her into his arms and she let herself sag. She crumpled against him, let his strength enfold her, and let him hold her as if her life force was spent.

It wasn't spent, though. This woman had the life force of a small army. She let herself be held for all of two minutes and then he felt her gather herself, stiffen, tug away.

And it nearly broke him. For those two minutes he'd felt her heart beating with his. He'd felt himself melt into her.

He'd realised what he'd lost.

'Thanks, Josh.' Her voice was still shaky but she was back to being professional—almost. 'That's what you don't see in most theatres—doctors cuddling doctors. But I was a bit woozy.'

'You didn't seem woozy when you were operating,'

Malu managed, and Maddie smiled and touched her patient's cheek. It was a gesture Josh knew—one of the things he'd noticed first about her. She was tactile, touching, warm.

He'd tried it out himself. It reassured patients. He'd learned from her.

Touching worked.

He wanted…

'I can pull myself together when I need to,' Maddie told Malu, and Josh knew her attention was back to where it ought to be—to her patient, to the situation—to her baby, lying peacefully on the air bed behind her. 'But now, if you don't mind, I'll let Dr Campbell take over my duty roster. Breathing easier?'

'You better believe it.'

'Excellent. That tube stays in place until we get an X-ray upstairs, but there's no blood coming out. That's a great sign. It means you have a slight tear in your lung but nothing major. As long as you stay fairly still—no need to make a martyr of yourself but let's not roll over without giving me or Josh forewarning—you should have no problems.'

'I'll need an operation when we get out of here?'

When? There was no if. Even though the walls around them were made of crumbling rock, Malu seemed to have forgotten.

That was down to Maddie, too, Josh decided. She was showing not one scrap of fear. If she'd been a doctor at the end of a long shift in an emergency ward of a large city hospital she couldn't be more composed. She was weary and she was signing off, but she was calmly reassuring her patient before she went.

I'll need an operation…

'You possibly will,' she told Malu. 'One of those ribs must have broken with a pointy bit. Josh and I don't like pointy bits, do we, Josh?'

'No, we don't,' Josh agreed gravely. 'But after what you've been through, an operation to stick two bits of rib together will be a piece of cake. You reckon you might go to sleep now?' With the amount of drugs on board it must be only the adrenaline of what had been happening—plus the terror of breathing difficulties—that had been keeping him awake.

'Going to sleep now,' Malu whispered, his speech already slurred.

'And you,' he told Maddie. He wanted to hug her again but she'd already turned and gathered her baby into her arms, transforming again into a mother. With baby. A brand-new family—of which he was no part.

He tugged an air bed to the far side of the shaft. 'Here,' he said, roughly because emotion was threatening to do his head in. 'Keanu's sent down sheets. Settle. I'll cover you all. You and Malu and Lea. And then you sleep.'

'Yes, sir,' Maddie said, still wobbly, and it was too much for Josh. He did gather her into his arms, but not to hold her as he wanted to hold her. Yes, his arm was weak. No, he shouldn't be doing any such thing, but he lifted her anyway, carrying her bodily across to the air bed, setting her down, making sure she and her baby were safe.

He covered them both with the sheet.

'I need to turn the torch off now,' he told her. Keanu had sent down more batteries but they were both aware that the line into their cavern was fragile and the time until rescue was unknown. They had to conserve everything. 'I'll lie beside Malu so I can feel if anything changes.'

'You're a wonderful doctor, Dr Campbell,' she whispered. 'Thank you.'

Him? A wonderful doctor… He stared down at her, speechless. But she closed her eyes and slept and he was left saying nothing at all.

CHAPTER EIGHT

THE NIGHT CREPT ON, inch by pitch-black inch. It was a relief that Malu needed checking. Every few minutes Josh flicked on the torch and checked the underwater seal, checked Malu's vital signs, checked there was nothing wrong with his patient—and then he checked Maddie.

He never shone the light directly at her. There was no way he was risking waking her. She slept the sleep of the truly exhausted.

Her baby lay in the crook of her arm as she slept. He'd suggested they use his air bed, setting tiny Lea up in a separate space, but the look she'd cast him had been one of disbelief.

'When the roof of the cave could come down any minute? She stays right by me.'

The baby care 'experts' would have a field day, he thought. Mothers in the same bed as their newborn? He'd heard a lecture once by a dragon of a professor...

How easy would it be for mother to roll onto her child?

It wouldn't happen. Every ounce of Maddie's being was in protective mode.

She was instinctively caring.

She was holding her daughter.

And all at once he was hit by a wave of longing so great it threatened to overwhelm him. Family...

He couldn't do family. Families hurt.

He flicked the torch off and settled back on his air bed. Not to sleep, though. Malu's obs were vital.

But things were okay. They were as safe as he could get them. He'd done what he could.

But suddenly things weren't okay. Things were very much not okay.

He was shaking—not just his arm this time, but his whole body.

Why? He was fighting to suppress what was going on, fighting to make sense of it.

He was exhausted—he knew he was. He'd been working on adrenaline for almost twenty-four hours. He was injured. His arm throbbed.

He'd helped his ex-wife deliver her baby. It made sense that it'd affect him. If he could put it into logic, then he could control it.

He'd had to stand back and watch while Maddie had operated. He'd been helpless. He'd lost control.

Think it through logically, he told himself. Keep it analytical. Stop the shaking…

He couldn't.

There was no sound, no movement, and yet he felt like the walls were caving in. His head felt like it was exploding. Sensation after sensation was coursing through him. Black fear… Maddie with rocks raining down around her. Lea with the cord round her neck. Malu gasping for breath…

And more. The past. A dying baby. Maddie lying in hospital, sobbing her eyes out. Looking down at the tiny scrap who could have been his son. A child who *was* his son.

And Holly, his little sister, lying still and cold in the mortuary. A little sister he'd protected and protected and protected.

Until he'd failed.

He couldn't breathe. He couldn't think.

This is a panic attack, he told himself, fiercely, but he couldn't listen. The doctor part of him, the part that had been his all for so long, the Josh who was a crucial member of Cairns Air Sea Rescue was no longer here.

He was a kid lying in the dark, alone and terrified, during the time he and Holly had been separated in two different foster homes. Where was she? What was happening to her? How could he keep her safe when they were apart?

And then…he was a guy bereft, looking down at the body of his tiny son. Seeing Maddie's anguish. Trying to figure how to hide his own anguish so he could help her.

And then Holly's death. Maddie trying to hold him. The cold, hard knowledge that he'd failed. He'd failed everyone.

He must have made some sound. Surely he hadn't cried out, but he couldn't stop shaking. He couldn't…

And suddenly Maddie was there, kneeling on his air bed. Tugging his rigid body close so his head was on her breast. Holding him, despite the rigid shaking, despite the fact that he didn't know why, he didn't know what…

'Josh…Josh, love, it's okay. Josh, we're safe.'

Her words made no sense. The sensation of losing control was terrifying.

Her words faded but her arms tightened.

She held, and there was nothing he could do but be held, to take strength from her.

For the first time ever?

It couldn't matter. He was so far out of control that to pull back was unthinkable. There was no strength left in him.

And gradually the tremors eased. She was kneeling on the air bed, holding him against her, running her fingers through his hair and crooning a little. And as the tremors eased, the crooning turned into words.

'Sweetheart, it's okay. We're safe. The nice men with the digging machines will get us out. This might not be the Ritz but we have comfy beds and Keanu's saying the pulley system's even good enough for hot coffee in the morning. Maybe that's what this is, love, lack of caffeine. You always were hopeless without coffee. But it's okay, Josh. We're all safe. Thanks to you, love, we're fine and we'll stay fine.'

And then she added a tiny rider, a whisper so soft he could hardly hear it.

'I love you.'

And the world settled on its axis, just like that. The tremors stopped. He was a man again. He was Dr Josh Campbell, being held by...his wife.

Needing comfort?

He didn't...need. How could he?

How could he not? It was like he was being torn in two.

He broke away, tugging back, just a little but enough to break the contact. She turned and flicked on the torch, not shining it directly at him but giving enough light to turn blackness into shadows.

She touched his face—and he felt himself flinch.

He raked his hair and then thought he shouldn't have done that. The feel of her fingers in his hair was still with him. He wanted it forever.

He couldn't have it.

To lose control... To stand at the edge of the precipice and feel himself falling...

'Maddie, I'm sorry. I'm...'

'What is it, love?'

Don't call me love. Somehow he stayed silent but he wanted to shout it. Why?

Because he wanted those barriers up. He was in control. He had to be. He knew no other way.

'Maddie, I don't know what happened.' He did, but there was no way he could open the floodgates, explain terror he hardly understood himself.

'This is scary.' She said it prosaically, stating the obvious for the idiot who didn't get it. 'You've spent the day being a warrior, but armour can only hold you up for so long.'

'Yeah.' Like that made sense.

What was he doing, being this feeble? Shame swept over him, a shame so deep it threatened to overwhelm him.

'Sorry.' He spoke more harshly than he intended and he forced his voice to moderate. 'Nightmare or something—who knows? I'm over it. I don't need—'

'Me?'

Yes, he wanted to say. It would be so easy to sink against her again, to take comfort. But beyond that... How could he survive if he needed her?

He couldn't.

'I guess I needed a hug,' he admitted.

'Of course you needed a hug. You're human, Josh. Giving works both ways.'

'But I don't need anything more.'

It was the wrong thing to say. He saw her flinch. 'Of course you don't.' She was watching him, with the expression of a woman who knew everything she needed to know about her man, and it made her sad.

'That's why we could never make it,' she whispered. 'You've never let me share your nightmares. You've never let me close.'

'I can't.'

'I know you can't,' she whispered with desperate sadness, and then Lea stirred and whimpered behind her and she turned away.

'Try and sleep,' she told Josh as she lifted her baby to her breast. 'We'll leave the torch on. I need it to feed and you need it to keep the nightmares at bay.'

'I don't need—'

'And maybe you never will and that's a tragedy,' she snapped. 'Think about it.'

Lea settled. Maddie gently rocked and crooned and loved.

And he lay there in the dark and he felt more lonely than he'd ever felt in his life.

He'd loved loving Maddie. He'd loved holding her, making her laugh, helping her, comforting her.

Wasn't it enough?

But as he watched Maddie's face, as he saw the peace settle over her as her tiny baby settled, he felt like a prism had opened into a world he hardly knew.

Cradling her baby helped. Cradling Lea brought Maddie peace.

She'd wanted to comfort him. The night Holly had died... He remembered coming out of the mortuary and Maddie had been there, white and shocked. She'd walked straight at him, gathered him into her arms and held.

And he'd pulled away. 'Go home, Maddie. There's no use for us both to suffer.'

To do anything else... To have let Maddie comfort him as she'd tried then...

It was still a precipice, and all he knew was to back away.

CHAPTER NINE

THE EXPERTS CHANGED their minds again. They didn't bore down from the top or the side; rather they cautiously picked their way through the existing shaft, inch by cautious inch, shoring as they came.

For those trapped, the wait seemed interminable, but they had what they most needed. Malu had stabilised and even improved. He slept.

Bugsy seemed resigned. He pinched half of Josh's air mattress. Josh used him as a pillow and he didn't mind. There was something comforting about using a golden retriever as a pillow. Josh slept fitfully while they waited, never for more than an hour at a time, keeping watch, but there seemed no drama. Maddie slept, too, waking only to feed and get to know her new daughter. If there wasn't the risk, Josh could almost imagine she was where she wanted to be. He watched the expression on her face as Lea's tiny mouth found the breast and suckled. He watched as Maddie's arms curved around her with love—and he was almost jealous.

Almost. He had himself back under control.

In the time he wasn't dozing, or attending to his little hospital's needs, he worked, and that was a relief. They now had netting above them, a sort of tent. He'd assembled it with care from materials sent in via the bags, small piece by small piece. It was made of wire mesh, and was supported by a series of triangular, snap-together poles. In the event of a full-scale collapse it'd be useless, but smaller loose stones were now less of a threat.

And the rescuers were on their way. Finally they could hear the miners through the rock.

'We reckon we're within six feet,' Keanu told him on one of their brief calls. Their supply of phone batteries was bearing up. The bag system could pull in more but the slightest rock slip could end their supply. Apart from that first indulgent baby parcel, only the barest essentials were coming in.

Malu was still drowsy but as the miners got closer Maddie stayed awake. Even Bugsy seemed restless. They all knew the last few feet were the most dangerous.

The more Josh thought about how he'd managed to get in here, the more he knew he'd been incredibly lucky—and maybe also incredibly stupid.

If Maddie hadn't been here…

Or not. Beth often told him he was crazy, that he had no fear, and maybe he didn't.

If there was an overturned car at the bottom of a cliff it'd be Josh who abseiled down to attend to an injured driver. He'd swung in a harness over a churning sea. He'd taken risks more times than he could remember.

Why not? It didn't matter if anything happened to him.

But now it mattered. He thought of the people dependent on Maddie and Malu. There were people outside who loved them.

'Do you have anyone back in Cairns you can hug when this is over?' Maddie asked into the silence, and he wondered if she'd been mind-reading.

'I… No.'

'No girlfriend?'

He thought about it before answering. He and Karen dated when it suited them. She was an adrenaline junkie, just like him, and for her birthday last month he'd taken her skydiving.

He remembered their dinner afterwards. She'd spent the night messaging about her awesome adventure to her mates.

No, he thought. She wasn't even his girlfriend.

'Earth to Josh…'

'Bachelorhood suits me.'

'That's fear talking.'

'Since when did you do psychology?'

'I had years to analyse you.'

'So why haven't you remarried?' he growled, and she snuggled down a little farther in her makeshift bed. Despite the earplugs they used during the worst of the drilling, the constant chipping of tools on rock was challenging.

Bugsy had abandoned Josh's air bed and was pressed hard against one side of Maddie, maybe sensing the increasing tension as the sounds of rescue grew closer. Lea was cradled in her arms. It was like she had a small posse of protection and he was on the outside.

'I tried marriage once.' She was speaking lightly, trying for humour, he thought. 'I don't have the courage to try it again.'

'So you'll raise your daughter on your own?'

'No.'

It was said sharply, and her words hung. For a moment he thought she wouldn't continue, but when she finally spoke her voice was reflective again.

'That's why I finally figured I could try again to have a baby,' she told him. 'When I realised I wasn't on my own. I guess…when I started working on Wildfire I was pretty much at rock bottom. I needed a job. The Australian government helps fund the medical services by supplying FIFOs. The pay's excellent and I was determined to keep Mum where she is. And, no, Josh, there was no way I was accepting help from you. But I hadn't been here for six months before I realised what a special place Wildfire is. The people are amazing, and the staff who are attracted to work here seem just as good. I guess all of us outsiders are running away from stuff, saving money, hiding, changing tracks... But the islanders welcome us all. Saying this place is like family sounds a cliché, but it's not.'

'That's why you ran into a collapsing mine?'

'Malu's wife is my friend. So, yes, in a way...'

'They're not your family.' He spoke more harshly than he'd intended. 'You're their doctor and colleague. They need you.'

'It works both ways. I need them.'

'How can you need them?'

'They accept me for what I am,' she said simply. 'When I ache, they ache. Last year Mum had another stroke. I went back to Cairns and had to stay for a month. When I came back, my tiny villa was a sea of flowers. Kalifa met me off the plane. Kalifa was one of the tribal elders, and he and his wife have practically been grandparents to me.'

She paused then and he knew she was thinking of the eldery man, of a needless death, and of who knew what else waited for them on the surface.

That's what happened when you got attached, he thought. It was like slicing a part of you out.

He didn't have that many parts left.

'I think Kalifa organised it,' she said softly. 'Or maybe it was his wife, Nani, or Pearl, Malu's wife, or Hettie or any one of so many... Anyway, all along the path to my villa were hibiscus, and I think I was hugged by every single Wildfire resident that night. And you know what?

That was the night I made the decision to have a baby. Because I'm part of a family. I'm loved and I can love back.'

The last few words were said almost defiantly. As if she expected him to reject them.

And then there was a sound of rubble, falling stones that made them both hold their breath. There was an oath from the far side of the rock and then the steady chipping restarted.

'I can't cope...with them putting their lives on the line for me,' Josh muttered.

'They're putting their lives on the line for all of us,' Maddie said, gentleness fading to asperity. 'You don't have a monopoly on heroism, Josh.'

'I don't—'

'No, that was mean.' She took a deep breath and winced again and he thought she was hurting. She'd given birth not twenty-four hours before. She'd already been bruised in the rockfall. Of course she was hurting. But she took a deep breath and kept on going. 'You know what I've figured?' she said, evenly again. 'I've figured that it's a whole lot easier to be the hero than the one dangling by her fingertips from the cliff.'

'What does that mean?'

'Why are you a doctor, Josh?' she asked, gently again. 'No, don't answer, because I know. It's because in medicine you can help. Add to that your search and rescue job and you can be the hero in every single situation. But when it comes to being rescued yourself, you can't handle it. That's what killed our marriage and it's killing you now.'

Silence. He watched her close her eyes and then saw her wince and put a hand to her neck.

Maybe there was something he could do.

'What's wrong?' he asked.

'Hero again?' she asked wryly, and she even managed a smile.

'Maddie, what is it?'

'I must have ricked my neck in the rockfall,' she confessed. 'I haven't had time to think about it.'

'Would a massage help?'

She thought about it. She looked at him for a long time in the shadowy light and then slowly she nodded.

'It might,' she said at last. 'But that'd mean accepting—again—that I need help.'

'You do need help. Maddie, being a single mother… You know it'll be hard. You still have your mother. You'll be doing a full-time job and trying to care for a baby, as well.' And then, because the sounds of rescue were growing closer and maybe there wouldn't be time to say it again, he said what he most wanted to say.

'Maddie, our marriage was good. The chemistry's still there. Maybe we can make it work again. Maybe we should try.'

'You'd be a father to Lea?'

'She needs a dad.'

'Need's no basis for a marriage. You must be the first one to tell me that.'

'But you need—'

'Josh, I don't need—at least, not from you. I have the community. I have my colleagues and my friends. Believe it or not, I even have my mum. She still loves me, even though she's so badly damaged, and her love supports me. I have everything I need. Marriage is something else. Marriage is for loving, not for dependency. It's for sharing and I don't think you ever will. I'm sorry, Josh, but I can't let you hurt me again.'

'I never would.'

'You don't understand how not to.' Then she smiled

again, trying desperately for lightness, trying desperately to put things back on a footing to go forward. 'But in terms of need... Okay, Josh, more than anything else, I would love a head and shoulders massage. You do the best and I've missed them. That's what I need from you, Josh Campbell, and nothing more.'

Why couldn't she give in to him?

She was giving in to him, she decided as his fingers started their magic. If this was the last massage he ever gave her, she'd enjoy every second.

She'd pretend he was hers?

The first time he'd done this to her had been just after she'd started work. He'd been waiting for her at the nurses' station. She'd been supposedly watching an operation but the surgeon had thought hands-on training was best. The surgeon had stood and watched every step of the way at what should have been a routine appendectomy.

Except it hadn't been routine. The patient had been a young mum with no history of medical problems, nothing to suggest the sudden, catastrophic heart failure that had killed her.

They'd had a cardiac team there in seconds, they'd fought with everything they'd had, but there'd been no happy ending. Maddie had walked blindly out of Theatre and Josh had been there. He'd gathered her into his arms and held.

He was good at caring was Josh. He was amazing.

They'd been supposed to be going out with friends. Instead, Maddie had found herself on a picnic rug on the beach, eating fish and chips, surprising herself by eating while Josh had let her be, just watched. And waited.

And then he'd moved behind her and started his massage.

It had started as gentleness itself, a bare touching, hands

placed softly on her shoulders, resting, as if seeking permission to continue.

She hadn't moved then. She didn't move now.

Permission granted.

And now his fingers started their magic.

First they stroked over the entire area he wanted to massage, her head, her shoulders, her back, her arms and her hands. She was resting against him but as his fingers moved she slumped forward a little, so he could touch her back.

Skin against skin.

How could he do this with an injured arm?

She couldn't ask. Maybe she couldn't even care?

Then his fingers deepened the pressure and she forgot what the question was.

He was kneading the tight muscles on either side of her neck, kneading upward, firm now, pressing into what seemed knots of tension. He worked methodically, focussing first one side then the other. His fingers kneaded, never so hard it hurt, never so hard she felt out of control, but firm enough to make the tension ooze upward and outward and away.

And then to her scalp. Her hair must be full of grit and sweat, a tangled mess, but right now she didn't care. Josh was stroking his thumbs upward, as if releasing the tension that had been sent up there by his wonder fingers. He was teasing her hair, tugging lightly, running his fingers through and through...

She was floating. She was higher than any drug could have made her. Lea was nestled beside her, Bugsy was at her other side, and Josh was turning her cavern of hell into one of bliss.

She heard herself moan with pleasure. She was melting

into him, disappearing into a puddle of sensual ecstasy…
His fingers… His hands…

Josh.

She drifted and he massaged and she floated, every single threat, every single worry placed at bay.

She loved… She loved…

And yet, as his fingers left her scalp and drifted down, beginning their delicious movements at her shoulder blades, an argument drifted back with them.

A long-ago conversation. After that night. They'd ended up in bed—of course. She'd slept through the night, enfolded by Josh's strong arms, and in the morning she'd woken to her beautiful man bringing her tea and toast.

'Where did you learn…?'

'One of my foster-mothers,' he told her. 'She used to have me do it for her after work.'

'Have you ever had anyone do it to you?'

'No,' he'd said shortly, and she'd set down her tea, looped her arms around his neck and drawn him to her.

'Well, I'm going to learn,' she'd declared. 'We'll massage each other every time we're stressed. Or even when we're not stressed. In fact, with massages like that, we need never be stressed again.'

He'd smiled and kissed her but then he'd drawn away. 'There's no need. I don't need a massage. Any time you want one, though…'

'So if I learn you won't let me practise?'

'As I said, sweetheart, there's no need.'

And there was that word again. It was like a brick wall, a solid divider that kept Josh on one side and the world on another. If he admitted need, then what? He'd fall apart?

She thought he'd crack. She thought if she loved him enough…

She was wrong.

He was stroking down her head now, across both her shoulders. There was grit on her shoulders and the remains of sweat and grime, but it made little difference. The finest oils couldn't have made her feel any more at peace than she was right now.

He was applying gentle pressure, running his fingers down her arms, using both hands, from shoulders to the tips of her fingers. She was totally subsumed by the sensation. If he wanted to make love with her right then…

Right… Less than two days after birth, in a collapsed gold mine, with her daughter, with an injured miner, with a dog…

The whole thing was fantasy. Her head was filled with a desire that could never be fulfilled.

His hands were stroking down her neck and shoulders, down her arms, breaking contact at her fingertips, over and over, but each stroke slower, slower, until finally his fingers trailed away from hers and held still.

Then a feather-light touch on her shoulders, a signal that it was finished.

Silence.

The end.

She wanted to cry.

She wanted to turn and hold him. She wanted to take him into her arms. She wanted him to be her…family?

She did none of those things. You couldn't hug a man with armour, she thought, no matter how much you might want to.

'Thank you,' she whispered into the shadows. 'Thank you, Josh, for everything.' And she gathered Lea back into her arms and held, not because Lea needed her—the baby was deeply asleep—but because she needed Lea.

'You need to sleep,' Josh said, and he held her shoulders while he moved sideways, so he wasn't right behind her, so she was free to settle back onto the air bed with her baby.

'Yes,' she whispered.

'Is there anything you need?'

'Nothing.'

Liar.

But it couldn't be a lie, she thought. She'd made her decision.

Or he'd made his decision years ago and nothing had changed.

And then a puff of dust surged out from the rocks above them and the dust had come from the gap Josh had used to get in, that they'd been using to haul bags back and forth.

'Anyone home?' There'd been scraping at the rocks that had grown so constant they'd hardly been listening—or maybe it was that they'd been just a bit distracted?

'Hey!' Josh called back, and his voice still sounded distracted. Maybe he was just as discombobulated as she was, Maddie thought, and was uncharitable enough to think, *Good!*

'I can see chinks of your light,' the voice called. 'You're eight feet away, no more. We've reinforced up to here. Another hour should do it. You guys almost ready to emerge?'

'You'd better believe it,' Josh said, but once again Maddie heard that trace of uncertainty.

It was as if they'd both be grateful to be aboveground, but neither of them was quite sure what they'd be leaving behind.

CHAPTER TEN

IT WAS MORE like three hours before the final breakthrough came, because no one was taking chances. By that time, however, there was a solid channel, a shored-up shaft that was deemed safe enough to risk moving them out.

They wasted no time. Safe was relative and any moment the ground could move again, so the move happened with speed. There was the moment's relief when a blackened face appeared, grinning and taking a second to give them a thumbs-up. Then there was skilled shoring work to make the entrance secure before a grimy rescuer was in the shaft with them and Maddie was being told she was to be strapped to a cradle stretcher, whether she willed it or not.

She didn't will it. 'Take Malu first.' She spoke it as an order, in her most imperious tone—a doctor directing traffic in the worst emergency couldn't have sounded more authoritative—and she couldn't believe it when she was overruled.

'Sorry, ma'am, orders are you're first,' the man said, and Josh touched her face, a light reassurance, but his touch was an order, too.

'They get two for the price of one with you,' he told her. 'You and your Lea. Lea's a priority, even if you're not. Off you go, the two of you.'

And then, because he couldn't help himself, he kissed

her, hard and fast, and it was an acknowledgment that being hauled out through the fast-made tunnel had major risks.

As if to emphasise it, another cloud of dust spat down on them.

'On the stretcher,' the man ordered, and Maddie had the sense to submit and then to stay passive, holding tight to Lea as what looked like a cradle was erected over her—the same shape as an MRI machine and just as claustrophobic. Once she was enclosed, the head of the stretcher was hauled up to the guy waiting, and she was lifted and pulled into the mouth of the shaft.

And then along. She didn't know how they did it. These guys were experts but she knew from their silence that they were working far closer to the limits of safety that they'd done before. And all she could do was lie still and hold Lea—and think of Josh left behind...

Josh, who didn't need anyone. Who'd be caring for Malu. Caring and never letting anyone care for him.

And then, amazingly, she was out of the darkness. The light was almost blinding and Lea was being lifted from her. She was being gathered into Hettie's arms and hugged and held, and Caroline was holding Lea and sobbing, and Keanu was there, giving her one fast hug, and she even saw tears in his eyes before he returned to his role as doctor.

They'd rigged up some sort of makeshift hospital tent. 'Let's get you inside,' he said roughly, trying to hide emotion. 'We need to assess—'

'I'm staying out here until the others are out,' she told him, and this time she managed to make them agree.

So Hettie organised washbasins and someone rigged up a sheet for a little privacy, and Hettie and Caroline did their midwife thing, as well as a preliminary assessment of scrapes and bruises, yet she could still see the mouth of the mine.

'She's perfect,' Caroline breathed, as she carefully washed Lea in one of the washbasins and inspected every part of her before wrapping her and handing her back to her mother. 'She's adorable, Maddie. Oh, well done, you.'

Surely Maddie should have beamed with maternal pride—and she sort of did but it was a pretty wobbly beam. She hugged her precious baby back to her, but still she looked at the mine entrance.

Malu's stretcher emerged next.

Keanu was ready to receive him, as was Beth. Hettie moved back to Keanu's side as well, so there was a receiving posse of medics moving straight into ER mode.

And, of course, Pearl was there. Pearl had greeted Maddie as she'd emerged, but even as she'd been hugging her, like Maddie, her eyes hadn't left the mouth of the mine.

As soon as the miners set Malu's stretcher down, Pearl was on the grass beside him, not saying a word, just touching his face, seemingly fearful of the drips, the oxygen mask, the medical paraphernalia Maddie and Josh had organised, but still...just touching.

And it was up to Malu to speak.

'Hey, girl,' he said, holding his wife any way he could. He spoke softly yet every person in the clearing could hear him. 'God help me, girl, I've needed you so much...' His voice broke on a sob and then, tubes or not, mask or not, everything was irrelevant, he was gathering Pearl into his arms and holding.

And Maddie couldn't help herself. Tears were coursing down her face. Happiness tears? There were matching tears on the faces of almost everyone around her, tears of relief, tears of joy, but mixed with that?

What sort of tears?

Jealous tears? To be loved like Pearl was. To be needed.

And then Josh was out, with Bugsy bursting out behind him. Josh had obviously refused the stretcher. He was bruised and battered. His arm needed urgent attention. She knew he'd lost strength so there was a chance of nerve damage, but he wasn't thinking of himself now. When was he ever? He stood blinking in the sunlight, gathering himself, and even as he did so Maddie saw him regroup, turn back into the professional, the doctor he'd become so he could help.

So he could hide?

But only she could see that. He saw her, half-hidden by sheets, lying in the shade, holding her baby. Their eyes locked for one long moment, a moment of recognition of all that was between them—and a moment of farewell?

And then he turned to Keanu.

'I'm fine,' he said roughly. 'We've got them out, now what else needs doing? Beth, what's the priority? What's the need?'

For once, however, Dr Joshua Campbell did not get things his own way.

Beth turned bossy. On his own turf he could have overruled her, but backed up by the island medical team of Keanu, Caroline and Hettie he'd met his match.

'No one needs you, Dr Campbell. In fact, for the duration you don't even consider yourself a doctor.' Hettie, the island's nurse administrator, was doing the organising. She looked to be in her late thirties and was obviously a woman to be reckoned with. Keanu was testing his arm, making him flex, testing each of his fingers. Together they gave him no choice.

They propelled him into the temporary hospital tent, whether he willed it or not. Malu was on the next stretcher.

Maddie was still outside.

Another of the nurses was at the door of the tent—Caroline Lockhart. She stood, looking a little unsure.

'Caroline?' Keanu said.

'The plane's due to land in twenty minutes,' Caroline told him. 'I've been talking to Beth. There's another doctor coming from Cairns to fly back with the patients. Beth says there'll be room for her and for two patients, but Pearl's desperate to go with Malu. She has a sister in Cairns she can stay with, and another sister here, who'll look after the kids. But a tropical storm's closing in over Cairns and they say this could be the last trip for a few days. If we need to send Josh then Pearl can't go.'

'I'm fine,' Josh growled. What were they doing, sending another doctor? Tending to patients during transport was what he did. 'You don't need another doctor from Cairns. I can care for Malu.'

'The doctor's already on his way,' Caroline said, ignoring his protest, talking to Keanu, not to him. 'And our little hospital's packed. Which leaves these two...these three, if you count Maddie's baby...'

'I'm fine,' Josh growled again, but no one was listening.

'Maddie wants to stay here,' Hettie said, still excluding him. 'She's looking good—there's no medical reason to evacuate her.'

'I'd like them both in hospital,' Keanu growled. 'All of them. Maddie and baby and Josh. Twenty-four hours' observation. The conditions underground weren't exactly clean and this is the tropics. Josh, this cut's deep and needs stitching. You get it infected, you risk long-term damage. The rest of your scratches need care and you need rest. So care it is. No one's growing infections on my watch.'

'Use the homestead,' Caroline said. 'You know we have

six bedrooms. I'll send a message to our housekeeper to make up beds. Keanu, you can do Maddie's obstetric checks there. Once you've done Josh's stitching and you're happy with them they should be fine. I can do obs.'

And Keanu stood back and looked at Josh—assessing. Seeing him not as a colleague but as a patient. Someone who needed help?

It was all Josh could do not to get up and walk out. To lie on the examination table and be assessed like this was almost killing him.

'I want gentle, gradual exercise,' Keanu said at last, still talking to Caroline. 'Slowly, no sudden movements. They've been cramped too long with injuries. So gentle movement with support, then food and bed. I'll give Maddie a thorough check first but if she's okay…I'll want them watched but the house should work. If we clear you from hospital shifts, you can look after them, and I can organise one of the night shift to take over while you sleep.'

'And act as chaperone, too.' That was Beth, standing at the entrance to the tent. She had her cheek back. When Josh had emerged from the mine she'd looked whey-faced but now she was practically bouncing. 'These two have been married,' she told the tent in general. 'Josh and your Maddie. Once there were sparks, so separate bedrooms at separate ends of the house.'

'I don't think we need to worry about these two and red-hot sex,' Keanu said dryly, and managed a grin. 'When two sets of bruises unite—ouch—and there's nothing like a one-day-old baby to dampen passion. However, they're consenting adults. Whatever they choose to do or not to do is up to them.' And then his smile widened, and Josh thought for the first time in two days the stress had come off.

'No, actually, that's not true,' Keanu added, still grinning. 'For now Maddie has no obstetrician so I'm it. So, Dr Campbell, no matter what your intentions may be regarding your ex-wife, could you please take sex off the agenda?'

'I have no intention...' He paused, practically speechless. Of all the...

'She's a lovely lady, our Maddie,' Keanu said. 'If I wasn't otherwise engaged I'd be attracted to her myself.'

'Hey!' Caroline said, and everyone laughed, and the tension lessened still further.

Except Josh's tension didn't ease. He was stuck on this island. He was about to spend the night in some sort of private house, even if it was a big one.

If he was at one end of the house and Maddie was at the other—she'd still be there.

No sex... There was no chance of that, but a part of him was suddenly remembering sex from a long time ago, how it had felt lying in Maddie's arms—how it had felt to be needed by Maddie.

That was the only time when his world had seemed right.

His world was right now, he told himself savagely. His world was exactly as he wanted it. All he needed was to get away from this island and get home.

Home? To his base in Cairns? An austere apartment he spent as little time in as possible?

He glanced around the tent at this tight-knit medical community, and then out through the tent flap to where a huddle of women crouched around Maddie. They were readying her for transport to the Lockhart house but this wasn't medical personnel doing their bit. These were friends, and even from here he could tell how much she was loved.

But not by him. He could never admit how much he needed her.

Not even to himself?

But this was exhaustion talking, he thought. This was nonsense.

'You'll be fine.' It was Hettie, washing his already cleaned face again, as if she knew that the grit felt so ingrained it'd take months to feel as if he was rid of it. 'We'll take care of you.'

'I don't need—'

'Need or not,' she said cheerfully, 'you're trapped until the storm front passes over Cairns, so you might as well get used to it.'

The bedroom was amazing. Luscious. Or maybe luscious was too small a word to describe it. 'It was my parents' bedroom,' Caroline had told her last night. 'Best room in the house.'

'Caro, I can't.'

'Of course you can.' Caroline had helped her shower and tucked her into bed, brooking no argument, and Maddie had been too overwhelmed to argue.

And now it was morning. She lay in a massive bed with down pillows and a crisp white coverlet, surrounded by delicate white lace that served as a mosquito net but looked more like a bridal canopy.

The bed was an island of luxury in a room that screamed of age and history and wealth. Old timber gleamed with generations of layers of wax and elbow grease. Vast French windows opened to the wide veranda beyond. White lace curtains fluttered in the warm sea breeze, and beyond the lagoon and then the sea.

Even her bruises thought they were in heaven.

She did ache a little, she conceded, but this was a bed, a room, a house to cure the worst bruises she could imagine.

And Caroline was standing in the doorway, holding her daughter.

'Sleepyhead.' Caroline chuckled as she set Lea into her mother's arms. At some time in the small hours she'd come in and helped Maddie feed—surely Maddie remembered that?—but the rest… How deeply had she slept? 'Your daughter's been fussing so I took her for a little stroll and introduced her to her world,' Caroline told her. 'She seems to approve. At least she seemed to approve until five minutes ago, when…'

As if on cue, Lea opened her mouth and wailed.

And Maddie felt her face split into a grin. There was nothing she could do about it—she couldn't stop grinning.

And Caroline smiled, too, as she helped Maddie show Lea to her breast—not that Lea needed much direction.

'Hmm,' Caroline said, standing back as Lea started the important business of feeding. 'I don't think you two will need breastfeeding advice.'

'I had a booklet I intended reading before she arrived,' Maddie told her, smiling and smiling down at her tiny daughter. 'Stupidly I left it behind when I went in, but Lea and I figured it out all by ourselves.'

'You left a lot else behind when you ran in,' Caroline retorted. 'Including all our hearts. Maddie, how could you?'

'How's Malu?' Maddie asked, answering Caroline's question with those two words.

'He's okay,' Caro conceded. 'Keanu had a call from Cairns a couple of hours ago. He's settled and stable and sitting up, having breakfast. Thanks to you and your Josh.'

'He's not *my Josh*.' She said it automatically. She was touching her tiny daughter's cheek as she suckled, and she was trying to think about Lea. Just Lea.

Only Josh was in her thoughts, too.

'He seems very concerned, for someone who's not *your Josh*.'

'Josh always cares,' she said carefully. 'It's what he's good at.'

'He wants to see you.'

'I'm sleepy.'

'You mean you don't want to see him?'

She thought about that for a moment. Of course she wanted to see him. She had to see him. After all, without Josh Lea would be dead. The thought made her feel… frozen.

If only he wasn't… Josh.

'How about breakfast first, a shower, maybe even a hair wash and then think about audiences,' Caroline suggested, with a sideways glance letting on that maybe she saw more than her words suggested. 'If I can tell him that, I may be able to bully him back to bed. He has a nasty haematoma on his thigh and Kiera wants him to stay in bed for the day.'

'A haematoma…'

'Cork thigh for the uninitiated,' Caroline said, and grinned. 'Honestly, don't you doctors know anything? He has a ripped and stitched arm, he's bruised all over and we know he hurts. So can I tell him if he's a good boy and stays in bed you'll see him before lunch? A ten-minute visit before you both go back to sleep?'

'Caro…'

'Mmm?'

There was silence while she thought of what to say. It lasted a while.

'He's stuck on the island?' she asked at last, and Caroline nodded.

'We all are. FIFOs are cancelled. Cyclone Hilda's hovering just above Cairns and the weather gurus don't know which direction she'll swing.'

'It's okay here.' There was safety in weather, she thought. It was the only discussion to be had when there was an elephant in the room so big it was threatening to overwhelm her. An elephant by the name of Josh. She made herself look out the windows to where the glassy calm of the lagoon and distant sea gave the lie to any hint of a cyclone. Still, it was the cyclone season...

'You're not really thinking of the weather, are you?' Caroline asked, and Maddie sighed.

'No.'

'So Josh is your ex-husband—only he's not acting like an ex-husband. Do you know how many orders he's throwing around about your care? If he could, he'd swim back to Cairns and swim back, dragging an obstetrician behind him.'

Maddie smiled at that, but absently. That'd be Josh. Caring above and beyond the call of duty. 'I'll see him before lunch,' she managed.

'Can I do your hair?'

'I don't need to be made pretty.'

'It never hurts.'

You have no idea, Maddie said, but she said it to herself, inwardly.

It never hurts?

It still did hurt—so much—after all these years.

She glanced down at her tiny daughter and she knew she needed all her strength and more if it wasn't going to keep hurting forever.

'Ten minutes and not a moment more,' Caroline told Josh as she escorted him along the vast, portrait-lined hallway to Maddie's room. 'Lea's just fed and Maddie is tired.

When I trained, it was the baby's dad and the baby's grand-parents—immediate family only—in the first twenty-four hours, and that's not you.'

It was said as a warning.

He stopped, which was a mistake. He'd been walking quite well until then. Caroline had wanted him to use a wheelchair. The idea was ridiculous but in truth his leg was weak and when he stopped he wobbled.

Caroline held out a hand to support him but he pulled back. What was happening here? Down the mine he'd coped well, apart from the brief and overwhelming panic attack, but on the surface he was suddenly as weak as Maddie's baby. He was wearing boxers and a T-shirt bor-rowed from Keanu. His own clothes were ruined, ripped and bloodied. He wanted jeans and a shirt that fitted, but Keanu had had the nerve to grin and tell him clothes would be forthcoming when he, Keanu, deemed Josh fit to leave this makeshift hospital and not before.

For once in his life Josh Campbell was out of control and he didn't like it. Not one bit. He didn't like it that his legs had the shakes—and now this woman was warning him about visiting Maddie.

Only family—and that's not you.

'I may not be family,' he said through gritted teeth 'but apart from a bedridden and confused mother, I'm all she's got.'

'You think so?' Caro said, quite lightly. 'Let me tell you, Dr Campbell, that if you step one inch out of line, if you upset Maddie enough to even make her blink, you'll find out this island is what she's got. The entire island and beyond. The whole M'Langi group. She's loved by us all. Family comes in so many forms.'

'That's not love,' he snapped. 'She's your local doctor. You people need her. She needs someone—'

'To protect her? That's what I'm saying, Dr Campbell. That's what she has. She ran into the mine to protect Malu but if you hadn't gone in after her I can think of over a dozen islanders who would have, including me. So let's not get carried away with heroics. Our Maddie might have needed saving in the mine, but she doesn't need saving from anything else.'

'Caro?' It was Maddie's voice floating down the hallway. 'What are you telling him?'

'Just normal midwifery stuff,' Caroline called out cheerfully. 'About not outstaying his welcome and new mothers need rest and not to cough anywhere near the baby. Oh, and there's antiseptic handwash on the bench...'

'He *is* a doctor,' Maddie called, and she was laughing.

'He might be a doctor where he comes from,' Caroline retorted, 'but from where I'm standing he's a patient wearing Keanu's boxers and learning to play by our rules.'

He was wearing boxers and a T-shirt. His dark hair was rumpled, tousled by sleep.

He had an ugly bruise on his thigh and his arm was wrapped in a stark white dressing.

He looked young, she thought, and absurdly vulnerable. She had a sudden urge to throw back the bedcovers and hug him.

He wouldn't let her. She knew it. Letting people close when he was vulnerable was not what Josh did.

She'd just finished feeding Lea. She cradled her close, almost as a shield.

'Hey,' he said, and she managed a smile.

'Have you remembered your antiseptic hand wash?'

He grinned back at her and held up his hands. 'Yes, ma'am. Do you think I dare disobey Commander Caroline? I stand before you, not a bug in sight—or out of sight, either.'

Oh, that grin. She remembered that grin. It did things to her.

Or not. Past history, she told herself fiercely. That grin could not be allowed to influence her in any way at all.

'How are you?' he asked, and it was as if he was holding himself back. He was still standing by the door. Unsure.

Maybe he wanted to hug her, too, she thought, and then she decided of course he did. Josh did comfort in a big way.

'We're both excellent,' she told him, cradling Lea close. Lea was still fussing a little, not hungry, just wide-eyed and not inclined to sleep. 'Me and Lea both.'

'What did Keanu say? Is he worried about infection? You tore a little. Has he put you on antibiotics? And how is Lea? I couldn't clean that cord stump properly. And has he checked both your lungs?'

'You know, if you're going to play doctor you need to find a white coat,' she told him. 'Boxers just don't cut it.'

'Maddie, I'm serious.'

'And so am I. Keanu's my doctor.'

'He's not an obstetrician.'

'Neither are you, though you did do a neat job of filling in,' she conceded. 'I wasn't too fussed about lack of white coats underground.' She smiled, forcing herself to stay light. 'But we're aboveground again now. Normal standards apply. We're both patients for the duration. Keanu's demanding I stay here for a week. I was due to fly back to Cairns today, but with Cairns airport closed I'm stuck. Caroline's been very kind.'

'It's her house?'

'It's her father's house, though it's been used by her uncle Ian. But until she came back a couple of months ago it's been empty. It seems Ian's done a runner. Apparently he's been ripping off money from everywhere. That's why the islanders were down the mine—they haven't been paid for months and they decided to do a bit of gold-mining for themselves.' She shrugged. 'But that's the island's problem, not yours.'

'But you care.'

'About the islanders? Of course I do.' She bit her lip. 'Kalifa died. He had no business...' And to her annoyance she felt tears welling behind her eyes. 'Damn, I'm as weak as a kitten.'

And Josh was over to her bed before she could begin to swipe the stupid, weak tears away, tugging her into his arms and holding. Lea was in there, too. He was cradling them both. His...family?

And it felt right. It felt like home. She could just sink into his shoulder and have her cry out, and let him comfort her as he'd comforted her so often in the past.

'Maddie, we could build again.' What was this? He shouldn't be speaking, she thought. She didn't want him to speak. This was Josh in his let's-make-things-better mode. Let's distract Maddie from what's hurting. She didn't want it but he ploughed on inexorably. 'We could make things right. Neither of us is happy apart. What you've done is extraordinary. You've rebuilt your life and I'm in awe. But, Maddie, I should never have walked away. I should have tried harder. I love you so much, and I love Lea already. We could buy a house with a view of the sea near the air rescue base. It's close to your mum. I can afford a housekeeper. It's near the base hospital, too, if you want to continue medicine. We could share parenting. We could start again.'

He was still holding her. She was still crumpled against his chest. She couldn't move.

She took time to let his words sink in. She needed to

take time. The last few days had left her hurt and shocked, and now... Josh's words felt like a battering ram, threating to crumble what was left of her foundations.

To calmly leave here... To go and live in Josh's beautiful house—she had no doubt he'd buy her something special... To have a housekeeper on call...

Share parenting, though... Was that a joke? That'd be where the housekeeper fitted in, she thought. Josh would be flitting in and out in between rescues, playing husband, playing father.

'You don't get it, do you?' she whispered, still against his chest because it was just too hard to pull away. 'You still want me to need you. You want us to need you.'

'What's wrong with that?'

And she did pull away then, anger coming to her aid. How could he be so stupid? How could he be so blind?

'Because love doesn't work one way,' she whispered, and then suddenly she was no longer whispering. She'd had five years to think this through, five years to know she was right. 'Love's all about giving. Giving and giving and giving. And how can I love you if all I can do is take?'

'I don't know what you mean.'

'Of course you do. It's why you walked away. Josh, after Mikey died, you tried to do it your way. You did all the right things. You said all the right things. You supported me every inch of the way. You stood by my side while we buried our son and your whole body was rigid with trying. You had to be everything to me. You couldn't crack yourself because I needed you. You couldn't show one hint of emotion, and you know why not? Because there's a vast dam of emotion inside you, and if you let one tiny crack appear then the whole lot will flood out, and you're terrified.'

'Maddie—'

'Don't "Maddie" me,' she bit out. 'You walked away

from me. Sure, you stuck around after Mikey died. You held yourself together, you hugged me and I let myself be hugged because, yes, I needed you, but it hurt even more that you didn't cry with me. You still hurt from losing Mikey. I saw it on your face when Lea was born but you won't admit it. You'll hardly admit it to yourself. And then Holly died and it was worse. You were wooden, as if admitting even a little bit of grief would make you implode. I was so sad for you, but when I tried to get close, when I needed to share, you walked away.'

Hell. He went to dig his hands into his pockets but boxers have a dearth of pockets. He felt exposed. He was exposed. Boxers and T-shirt and bruises and…emotion.

'It was five years ago,' he managed. 'It's history.'

'You mean you have your armour back in place so we'll start again? That'll be fine as long the need all stays one way.'

'Maddie, you care for your mother. You'll care for Lea. You don't need—'

'Another person who needs me? That's what I mean. You still don't get it. Not letting me close hurts, Josh. After five years I should have built my own armour but I don't want to build armour. I love it that my mum needs me. I love it that Lea needs me and I love it that I have a working life where this community needs me, too. But you know what? I need them, too. I sit and read to Mum and it warms my heart that she can still smile and hold my hand. I cradle Lea and I'm warm all over. The islanders bring me their problems but they also include me in their lives. They share, and when I'm off the island I miss them. Kalifa died when the mine collapsed and I'll go to his funeral and I'll weep. I loved him. I needed him as I need so many.'

'You can't—'

'Don't tell me what I can and can't do, Josh Campbell. You don't have the right.'

And suddenly she was almost shouting and Caroline was gliding into the room and putting herself firmly between Josh and Maddie and giving him a glare that might have turned lesser mortals into stone.

'What do you think you're playing at?' she demanded. 'I told you—you upset Maddie, you upset the whole island. Maddie, you want me to call in a few good men to cast this guy to the fish?'

'I... No.' Maddie choked on an angry sob and fell back on her pillows. Lea whimpered and Josh felt sick.

'What's he been saying?' Caroline demanded. 'Tell Aunty Caroline.'

'He wants to marry me—again.'

There was a moment's stunned silence. Then Caro's lips twitched. It was a tiny twitch. She had herself under control in an instant but he saw it.

'So he proposes in Keanu's boxers and T-shirt,' she managed. 'I can see why that would upset a girl. And where's the diamond?'

'I don't want a diamond.'

But Caroline had moved back into professional mode. 'What you want,' she said, lightly now but still just as firm, 'is a sleep. I'm going to take your obs and then close this room off to everyone. Whatever Dr Campbell has been saying, forget it. What's most important, for you and for baby, is sleep.' And then she lifted Lea from Maddie's arms and turned and handed the tiny girl to Josh.

'Here,' she said, and Caroline might be young but right now she was every inch a Lockhart of Wildfire, with a lineage obviously stretching back to the dinosaurs. No old-fashioned hospital matron had ever sounded more bossy. 'Lea looks like she needs time to settle,' she decreed. 'I need to care for Maddie and if you're proposing marriage then maybe you could take this small dose of domesticity and try it out for size. Keanu wants you to walk, just a little, slowly but getting the circulation moving in those legs. We don't want clots, do we? Can you hold her without hurting your arm? Excellent. I want you to take Lea for a wee walk around the veranda, then settle down outside until I come and get her. You're banned from here, Dr Campbell. Now, Maddie, do you need some pain relief? Yes? Let's get you sorted.'

And she turned her back on Josh, blocking his view of Maddie.

He was left with an armful of baby.

He was left with no choice but to leave.

CHAPTER ELEVEN

HE STOOD IN the hall, holding Maddie's daughter, and he thought…

Nothing.

Maddie's words were still echoing in his head. He should try and make sense of them, but he couldn't sort them out.

In his arms Lea wuffled and opened her mouth to wail.

And at that, the professional side of him kicked in. Caroline had given him Lea for a reason. She knew he was more than capable of caring for a baby. She also knew that Maddie was distressed and needed to sleep, and the one thing that'd stop her doing that was to hear her baby crying. That was the reason she'd handed her over to him. Professional concern.

So be professional. How to stop a baby crying?

He hadn't actually read that in any of his textbooks.

Still, it was a professional challenge and he was a professional. How hard could it be?

'Hush,' he told Lea, and he lifted her onto his shoulder and let her nuzzle into the softness of his T-shirt while he made his way outside.

He walked for a little, as ordered, until the threat of wails was past, until he heard only gentle wuffling. Then he headed for a mammoth rocker on the side veranda. He settled—cautiously—into the softness of its faded cushions, and rocked.

It was a good place to sit. There were herons wading at the edge of the lagoon, seeking tiny fish in the shallows. The veranda was shaded, cool and lovely. In the distance the sea was a sheet of shimmery, turquoise glass.

There was a cyclone threating Cairns, but here there was nothing but calm.

'There's no threat here,' he murmured to the baby in his arms, but she seemed singularly unimpressed.

She whimpered some more. He lifted her from his shoulder and cradled her in his hands. Why did newborns feel so fragile? He knew from training that babies were born tough but she didn't feel tough.

She felt precious.

He laid her on his knee. He expected to hurt a bit as her weight settled on his bruised thigh, but she nestled as if this was a cradle made for her. Her eyes were drifting with newborn lack of focus but she seemed to be taking in this strange new world.

She looked like Maddie.

Who was the father? he wondered. Who was the unknown sperm donor?

He wished it could have been him.

No. He didn't wish that. Fatherhood… He remembered clearly the agony of loss.

His son and then his sister.

How could he hold himself and not crack? That's why he'd had to walk away. He couldn't help Maddie when he was hurting so much himself. He was no use to anyone.

'If you were mine I'd be useless,' he whispered. 'If you hurt… Or if your mother hurt…'

So why had he offered marriage again? What had changed?

Hope that this time it could be different? Hope that there wouldn't be a time when he was needy?

'Excuse me?'

He turned to see a woman maybe in her late sixties standing at the foot of the veranda. She was short, slightly overweight, breathless. Her soft, white hair was tugged into a wispy bun and her eyes looked swollen, like she'd been crying.

'Excuse me,' the woman said again. 'I knocked on the front door but no one answered.'

'I'm Dr Campbell,' he told her. 'Can I help?'

She'd been climbing the side steps, but as soon as Josh spoke she stopped short, looking at him in shock.

'You're a doctor?'

'I don't look like one, but yes.'

'So…Keanu said…you were helping when my husband died.'

It was a simple statement, said with dignity and peace, like a jigsaw puzzle was coming together in a way she could understand.

'You're Kalifa's wife,' he ventured, remembering the big man, the desperate fight to save him, the hopelessness he always felt when he lost a patient. He'd been gutted, and then the trauma with Maddie had stopped him following up. Normally when a patient died in his presence he'd seek out the relatives and talk them through it.

Too much had happened.

'Kalifa Lui was my husband,' the woman agreed, look-ing to the baby, to him, then back to Lea. 'My name is Nani Lui. The nurses told me that you and Keanu tried very hard to save him. I thank you.'

'I wish we could have done more.'

'It would seem that you've done more than you could be expected to do,' she said, and the echo of a smile washed across her tired face. 'Did they teach you mine rescue in medical school?'

But then she was interrupted. 'Nani?' It was Maddie, calling through the open window. 'Nani, is that you?'

Uh-oh. 'You're supposed to be asleep,' Josh called back. 'We'll move farther along. Caroline will have us hauled before the courts for disturbing you.'

There was a sleepy chuckle. 'Caroline's gone across to the hospital to get more diapers and, oh, I need to see Nani. Quick, Josh, bring her in.'

'Nani, if you go through that door…'

'No,' Maddie called out, suddenly imperious. 'Come in with her, Josh. I want Nani to meet both you and my daughter.'

He was wearing boxers! 'I'm hardly dressed—'

'Nani won't care. She's practically family and I guess… after all we've been through, so are you.'

So he ushered the elderly woman into Maddie's bedroom—keeping a wary eye on the door. Caroline seemed a woman it was better not to cross. But Maddie's distress seemed to have evaporated. She hugged Nani to her as Josh had seen her hug her mother and he thought…maybe it was true. Maybe Nani was family.

He stood silent, feeling superfluous, until the hugging finished, until Nani stepped back, tears streaming down her face, and turned back to see Lea in Josh's arms.

'And this is your little one,' she whispered. 'They tell me you've named her Lea. For my daughter?' She forced her gaze from the baby to Josh. 'Lea was my daughter,' she whispered. 'She did the cooking at the hospital. She was so full of love and laughter. Then she got the encephalitis. It was so bad, so fast. Maddie worked desperately to try and save her but she died before she could be evacuated. And now… To call your little one for her… My Kalifa would be so proud.'

And Josh looked down at Maddie and saw her eyes fill with tears. It was true, then. She'd named her baby for a patient she'd lost.

Part of her extended family? Surely not. He hadn't asked, though…

He hadn't had the right to ask why she'd decided to call her baby anything.

It hurt that he didn't have that right. It hurt a lot.

'She's beautiful,' Nani whispered. 'A new life from this tragedy. This is joy. And you called her Lea.'

'I wanted to share.' Maddie's voice was weak but determined. 'I know all of you will love her. She'll need you all.'

'And we'll need her,' Nani breathed. 'Oh, Maddie, I'm so happy for you.' She glanced up at Josh. 'Maddie's wanted this little one for so long.'

'I know.'

And Nani's gaze sharpened. She looked from him to Maddie and back again. 'It's true then,' she said forcefully. 'They're saying you two were married.'

'I… Yes.'

'And you walked away.' Her tone was accusing.

'I couldn't help her,' Josh said helplessly.

'Maddie said she couldn't help you.'

'Maddie talked to you about us?' He turned to Maddie, incredulous.

'I'm a grandmother,' Nani said simply. 'Everyone talks to me.' And then she paused, the present crashing home. 'But not my Kalifa. No more. People tell me things and I weep for them, but then my Kalifa holds me…'

'We'll hold you, Nani,' Maddie said. 'You know we will. Whenever you need us. Just as you've always held us.'

And Nani's face crumpled. She stooped and hugged

Maddie and she sobbed, just once. And then she sniffed and braced herself and rose and faced Josh again.

'She will, too,' she said. 'Maddie is part of my strength, part of this island's strength. I knew Maddie would be sad about Kalifa's death. She told him to stop smoking. She told him to lose weight. He didn't listen but she tried, and she was there for him when he needed her. As she always is.'

She stopped and stared down at the tiny child and her face softened. 'Life goes on,' she whispered. 'With no blame. With love. This little one…she's our faith in the future. She gives me strength, and, heaven knows, we all need to take strength where we can find it.'

'You find it in yourself,' Josh said, and Nani stepped back and looked at him as if he'd said something that didn't make sense.

'Is that what you think? That you're born with strength enough to hold you up for your whole life?' She groped backwards and sat and held Maddie's hand. 'Is that what drove you apart?'

'Maybe,' Maddie said, and Josh heard exhaustion in her voice.

'We shouldn't be here,' he told Nani. 'Caroline will be after us with a shotgun if she finds us in here. Maddie, go to sleep, love.'

'I'm not your love,' Maddie whispered, and Josh flinched.

But what she said was true. He might love Maddie. She might love him but the chasm between them was still miles deep.

He ushered Nani out. Nani looked as if she was bursting to say more but she held her tongue. Out on the veranda she touched Lea's face again and then gave Josh a searching look.

'There's time,' she said enigmatically. 'You can't be the only one to take care of you.'

She left. Josh looked down at the baby, now sleeping soundly in his arms. He thought of the web of love and dependence and need that held this island together.

He thought he'd head back to his rocker.

Babysitting was easier than thinking, he decided. It was just a shame he could do both at the same time.

She wasn't asleep. She was tired and drowsy, her body was as comfortable as Caro could make it and there was no reason she shouldn't sleep, but she lay in her beautiful bed and looked out at the distant sea and thought about Josh.

He was on the veranda. He'd be rocking back and forth, looking out over the lagoon.

Holding her baby.

He'd called her 'love'. He still wanted her. He even wanted marriage.

The idea was preposterous, crazy, even heartbreaking, so why was there an insidious voice hammering away in her consciousness?

Go on. You know you want to.

And part of her did want to. Despite what Nani had said, this island wasn't her all.

There was still a part of her that ached for Josh.

Down the mine he'd massaged her head and shoulders, and, despite the shock, the danger, the physical battering her body had just been through, his touch had swept back all the memories of the fire between them. He just had to look at her and her knees turned to jelly.

Lovemaking with Josh.

There was a memory she had to suppress. It was still there, though. The perfection.

Five years. Surely she should have moved on by now?

The problem was that she'd made vows.

With my body I thee worship.

Had she made that vow? For the life of her she couldn't remember. Her wedding day had passed in a blur of happiness, and the words she'd spoken, with love and with honour, had blurred, as well.

With my body I thee worship.

If she hadn't said it out loud, she'd said it in her head.

It wasn't enough. It had never been enough. Not when the caring was only permitted one way.

If Josh loved, he protected, and protection for Josh meant never letting her close enough to see his hurt.

'It's impossible,' she whispered into the stillness. 'The island has to be enough. I can't love a man who won't let me love back.'

The only problem was that she did.

'Josh?'

He'd been dozing a little, the rocking chair stilling as he and Lea drifted towards sleep. His legs made a secure cradle. His hands still cupped her. Lea was peaceful and seemingly content, and for this moment so was Josh.

He had to be. Listening to Nani had left him…discombobulated. He'd tried to figure it out but the effort had left him too tired to sort the tangle that was in his head. For now all he could do was soak in the sun, the peace, the feel of this little girl sleeping between his hands.

Everyone should have a Wildfire Island, he thought sleepily. And a baby called Lea.

'Josh!' It was Caroline again—of course. She was standing in front of him, smiling her approval. 'What a great job,' she told him. 'We'll give you a job in the children's ward any day.'

'Do you have many ill children?'

Why did he ask that? Because he wanted to shift the focus onto medicine? Okay, maybe he did. Ever since he'd arrived on this island, things had been personal and it was time to back away.

'We have too many ill children,' Caroline told him, obviously ready to follow his lead. 'As well as normal kids' stuff we have a vicious ulcer caused by the local mosquitoes. It starts out as a mosquito bite and grows. If left untreated it needs to be cut out and requires skin grafts. What's worse, we also have encephalitis caused by the same mosquito. There's a local remedy—a plant that seems to give immunity—but sometimes parents forget how important it is to use it. We aim to send the encephalitis patients to the mainland but that's not always possible. In the meantime, we need to do the front-line treatment here and the cases are increasing. The island's desperate for more medical staff but there's no money. The government funding's limited and we're running out. And now the encephalitis cases are increasing.'

'Why?'

'Because the money's run out, for education and also for mosquito eradication,' she said bitterly. 'My uncle seems to have been embezzling funds for years. Heaven knows how we can attract any more staff. We're just blessed that Maddie's decided to stay.'

And he'd asked her to leave.

But for her to stay here... With Lea...

Ulcers. Encephalitis...

'You needn't worry. We take very good care of our staff,' she said, seeing him glance at the sleeping baby and guessing his concern. 'And our staff's children. This baby will be cared for by the whole island. But that's not what I came to talk to you about. Keanu's just had a call from Cairns Air Sea Rescue. From Beth. She says to tell you the

cyclone's tracking north and the airport's open from dawn
tomorrow. So, unless you don't want it, they're flying out
to collect you. She wanted to know if Maddie wants evacuation, too, but Maddie's adamant that she stays. Keanu
doesn't see any reason why she shouldn't. Oh, and the
plane's bringing our permanent doctor back, Sam Taylor,
so we'll have a full medical contingent again, or as full
as we can afford. Can you be ready to leave at ten tomorrow? Keanu's trying to find you some decent clothes to
wear on the way home.'

Unless you don't want it.

In all that she'd said, those were the words that stood
out.

Ten tomorrow morning, unless he didn't want it.

His boss would insist he take a break, he thought, at
least until the cut on his arm healed. He could…

What? Stay here?

What was the point? He'd only upset Maddie.

'Of course,' he said, and the matter was decided.

She left, taking Lea with her. He stayed sitting on the
rocker, staring sightlessly out over the island.

What was the point?

He'd rescued Maddie. He'd played emergency doctor
because that was what he did. That was who he was. There
was no use pretending he could be anything more.

It was time to move on.

At nine the next morning, Maddie had just finished feeding when there was a knock on the door.

'Come in,' she called, and it was Josh. Of course it was.
Caroline had told her he was leaving. She'd warned her
he'd want to say goodbye.

He was wearing clean jeans and a crisp, short-sleeved
white shirt. He was washed and brushed and almost im-

possibly handsome. He looked like Josh again. If it hadn't been for the dressing on his arm she'd say he was back to being her invincible Josh. No, not *her* Josh. *The* Josh. The Josh who was in control.

'Caroline says if I promise not to upset you I can have ten minutes,' he said, and part of her wanted to say he could have the rest of her life. But she was sensible and there was no way a sensible woman could say such a thing. Even if he looked like Josh.

'I won't get upset,' she managed. 'You'll be glad to get back to work.' Of course he would. An idle Josh was like a bear with a sore head. Or a sore arm? 'Will they let you work with that arm?'

'Office duties.'

'You won't take a holiday?'

'No.'

'You need to rest.'

'Says you. Are you sure you don't want us to take you to Cairns?'

'I'll go in a week or two, when I'm recovered,' she told him. 'I need to see Mum, but I can't for a little while yet.'

He understood. She couldn't push a wheelchair. She couldn't spend a whole day with her mum.

'I'll go and see her if you like. I'll send word back.'

'That'd be…kind. She'll remember you. She I—'

But then she bit back the word. *Loved.* It was too big to say, and Josh was moving on.

'Going back and forth to Cairns will be hard with a baby.'

'It won't be.' Her chin tilted, a gesture he knew and loved. His brave Maddie. 'It'll be the same as before, only this time I'll have Lea, too. I'm thinking Mum will love her.' And she did say the L word then.

'Maddie, how can you manage?'

'How I can is none of your business,' she said, gently but firmly. 'I'm not asking you to care. In fact, I'm asking you not to care. You've cared before and it almost broke you. You walked away from our marriage because of it and nothing's changed. Lea and I have nothing to do with you, Josh.'

'Yet…'

'There are lots of yets,' she murmured. 'But none of them work.'

'I love you.'

'Not enough.'

'Maddie…'

'When Lea cries, I'll comfort her,' she said, trying to make sense of what didn't make sense at all. But it did—in a stupid, muddly way. 'And you know what? She'll comfort me back. Oh, she won't—she can't—care for me. Even in old age I hope she won't need to care for me, but she'll hug me and she'll be there and just knowing I'm her mum, knowing I'm loved, that's enough. I won't ask for more. But to be there for her when she hurts? What a privilege to be permitted to be so close to someone. And when I hurt and she hugs me…that's a gift, too. A gift you could never accept.'

'You know I can't.'

'I know you can't,' she said, sadly now, and she hugged Lea tightly. 'All I can do is hope that one day you'll meet a woman strong enough to crack that armour.'

'Maddie—'

'It's time to go, Josh,' she said, and her bottom lip wobbled a bit. 'It's over.'

Only it wasn't. He stooped as if compelled. He put his hands on her shoulders and he bent so his eyes met hers.

And, as if she was compelled in turn, her face tilted to

meet his. Her eyes were wide, her lips parted, just slightly, in just the way he remembered.

And he kissed her. Properly this time, not like the kiss they'd shared in the darkness and the stress of the mine.

Some things were the same.

Some things were mind-blowing.

He remembered the first time he'd kissed her, the sweetness, the taste, the rush of heat. He remembered the way his body had responded—like here was the other half of his whole.

He remembered thinking it must be something in the water—or what they'd eaten. It had been their first date. They'd bought hamburgers and eaten them on the beach at sunset.

They'd kissed and when they'd finally drawn apart he'd felt like his life had just changed.

He remembered thinking it was ridiculous. She was a colleague. She was just someone…nice.

Nice hadn't come into that kiss.

Nice didn't come into this kiss.

The heat was still there, and the power.

Two bodies, fusing.

They might just as well be naked between the sheets. This kiss said they knew each other as they'd know no other.

Two becom one? They'd made their wedding vows but vows didn't come into this. It was the way he felt.

It was the way she made him melt.

Her lips were parted and the kiss she gave him was all Maddie. Generous. Holding nothing back.

She was soft and strong, warm and wanting.

She gave everything.

He remembered that about her. Her love for her mother. Her generosity to her friends.

The way she gave her body to his.

He'd thought he could lie with this woman forever. He thought he'd found his home, and somehow it was still here, this sweet, perfect centre. This aching, loving perfection.

Her kiss said it all. Her hands were in his hair, tugging him to her, kissing him back with a passion that made his heart twist. That made him want to gather her into his arms and carry her.

To where?

To where he could protect her forever?

She must have felt the discordant note, for suddenly the fierce hold eased and she was pushing him back. When their lips parted he felt as if their bodies were being wrenched apart, but she was smiling.

Sort of. He knew this woman. He could see the glimmer of tears behind the smile. But he could also see the strength—and the decision.

'Time to go, Josh. If I ever need rescuing again you'll be the first person I call on, I swear.'

'I'll come.'

'And if you need rescuing?'

Silence. Her smile stayed, but there was infinite sadness behind it.

'If ever you change your mind…' she whispered. 'If ever you want to hop off your white charger and let me have a turn…' But then she bit her lip. 'No. I won't make a promise like that. I've tried to move on, and I'll keep trying. You go back to your life, Josh Campbell, and I'll stay here with mine.'

'Maddie…'

'No more words,' she whispered, and put a finger to his lips, a feather touch, almost a blessing. 'Just go.'

He was gone.

She lay in her too-big bed and hugged her baby. Her body ached.

Her heart ached.

She'd made the right call—she knew she had—but, oh, it hurt. And it was hurting Josh, too.

'Impossible,' she murmured to herself, but then Lea wriggled and opened her eyes and screwed up her nose and told her mother in no uncertain terms that all was not right with her world.

She was a mother and she was needed.

'But not by Josh,' she told herself. 'I'm on my own.'

Only she wasn't. She had her baby. She had her mother, her friends, the islanders.

It was only Josh who was alone, she thought bleakly.

He had no choice. With the demons he was carrying he'd stay alone forever.

CHAPTER TWELVE

'I'M NOT LYING on any stretcher.'

'Honey, we came to pick you up on the grounds that you're a medical evacuation,' Beth told him. 'If we told the powers that be you're fine, apart from a gashed arm, you'd be told to have a nice holiday on Wildfire and come back with the supply boat next week. But you've a gashed arm, a haematoma and shock. Post-traumatic stress disorder is yet to be ruled out. Lie down, like a good boy, and let me give you an aspirin.'

'I'm not lying down,' he said, revolted, and she raised her brows.

'Um…I have backup. The medical opinion on your bruised leg is that sitting upright for the flight is asking for clots and you're not growing clots on my watch. You lie down or we land again and I'll have Sam and Keanu come in here and sit on you. Straitjacket if necessary.'

'You wouldn't dare.'

'Try me,' she said, and grinned and crossed her arms and kept her brows raised. 'Down!'

He had no choice. He lay on the stretcher. She smiled and strapped him in.

'Mind, we could have left you there,' she said serenely. 'We gave you that option.'

'There's no point.'

'Maddie's moved on?'

'I… Yes.'

'Funny things, marriages,' she said. 'Unless they end really bitterly, you always leave a bit of your heart behind.'

'I haven't.'

'No?'

'No,' he said, and then decided if he was to be treated as a patient he could act like a patient. He lay back and closed his eyes as the plane raced down the runway and took to the skies.

He'd have kind of liked to sit up and look down at the disappearing islands behind him.

Saying goodbye hadn't been enough.

It had to be enough. They'd go back to Christmas and birthday cards and that'd be it.

You always leave a bit of your heart behind.

Philosophy of Beth, he thought dryly. After two marriages and four sons, she had an opinion on everything.

She was wrong this time. It wasn't a bit of his heart. It was a lot.

No. It was the whole box and dice. He lay back with his eyes closed, and it felt like he was leaving a part of himself down there. It wasn't just Maddie, either, he thought. He'd delivered Lea. He'd cradled her in his big hands and he'd felt…he'd felt…

Like she was his?

She wasn't, though, and neither was Maddie.

They could have been his wife and his daughter.

He'd walked away.

And all of a sudden it was just as well he was lying down, as the sweep of emotion flooding through him might have sent him reeling.

He wanted them with a fierceness he'd never experienced before. He wanted to be part of their lives.

He wanted his marriage back.

Marriage… In sickness and in health. Why did that line suddenly slam into his head?

Because he remembered Maddie saying it. To love and to honour, in sickness and in health.

He'd said the words as well, and he'd meant them.

But he hadn't let Maddie mean them.

He'd met Maddie just as her mother had suffered her stroke; when Maddie had been in distress. He'd been able to help. He'd been strong, capable, ready to move heaven and earth if it could make Maddie smile again.

He'd loved helping her and he'd fallen in love.

Because she'd needed him?

Why should he have these insights now, after all these years? It was impossible to understand, and suddenly his thoughts were everywhere.

He remembered the night Mikey had died, trying desperately to hold on to his rigid control. 'It's okay to cry,' Maddie had said, more than once, but he hadn't. He'd held her while she'd broken her heart, and then he'd walked off his pain and his anger where she hadn't had to see.

His job was to protect.

And then, five months later, the policemen at the door. *Your sister, sir…*

He remembered Maddie moving instinctively to hold him, to take him into her arms, and yet he'd backed away.

He'd failed even more. He couldn't protect his sister. He couldn't protect his wife.

They'd been in the air for over half an hour now. Back on Wildfire a funeral would be starting.

Kalifa Lui. Nani's husband.

His thoughts were flying every which way but suddenly they were centred on Nani. Mourning her husband but finding the strength to visit Maddie.

Nani, touching Lea's face, taking strength from a baby. Maddie, taking strength from Nani.

Loving was all about giving? That had been his mantra, but in Maddie's world loving worked two ways. Giving love and receiving love. Giving comfort and receiving comfort.

Just loving, no strings attached.

Maddie would be at the funeral now, he thought. No matter how sore, no matter how much she'd prefer to be in her magnificent bed with her sea view and her beautiful baby, she'd be at the funeral and no one would send her away.

There'd be no objection from Nani. He knew it. Nani knew that accepting love was the same as giving it.

To accept love wasn't a weakness?

To accept love might even be a strength.

How had it taken so long for him to see it? Was he stupid?

Could he admit he'd been stupid? More, could he act on it?

His thoughts washed on. He lay so silent that finally Beth moved from her seat to check on him.

'Don't you dare die on my watch,' she told him. 'We're only an hour from Cairns.'

'No, we're not.'

'Not?'

'No.' He was trying to unclip the straps holding him in place. 'Give me the radio.'

'What? Why?'

'This is a medical emergency,' he told her. 'I believe Maddie is attending a funeral without proper medical attention. She needs an emergency physician.'

'You're kidding.'

'I would never kid about anything so serious,' he told her. 'But this isn't your decision.'

'Josh…'

And then he softened. Start now, he told himself. Share.

'Beth, I'm in love,' he told her. 'I've been stupid and blind and any number of adjectives you want to call me, but I'm over it. I need your help.'

'You?' she said in disbelief. 'You need my help?'

'I need your help,' he said humbly. 'Dear Beth, please help me unfasten these straps and hand me the radio. And then let's get this plane back to Wildfire.'

The day thou gavest, Lord, has ended, the darkness falls at thy behest…

If there was one thing the islanders of M'Langi prided themselves on it was singing, and the combined voices of what seemed at least half the population was enough to bring tears to Maddie's eyes.

Actually, there were a few things bringing tears to Maddie's eyes right now.

First and foremost was that Kalifa had been a friend and he'd died too soon. If he'd been sensible, stopped smoking, lost weight—if he hadn't decided to embark on a hare-brained scheme to make money out of a patently unsafe gold mine—she wouldn't be standing here.

Then there was the sight of Nani, surrounded by her children and her grandchildren. It'd be desperately hard for Nani now, she thought. The elderly woman lived out on Atangi, the biggest of the island group, but her children mostly lived on Wildfire.

She had no money. Kalifa had given it all to his son after he'd lost his fishing boat. He'd mortgaged their house and Nani would have no hope of redeeming it.

She'd lost her husband and her home, yet her shoulders were straight, she sang with fierce determination, and Maddie looked at that sad, proud woman and felt tears well again.

And then there was Josh. Gone.

He'd left five years ago, she told herself. One visit and here you go, falling in love again.

Or still loving?

It's just hormones, she told herself fiercely. She'd given birth only three days ago. Caroline was on one side of her and Hettie was on the other. They both thought she shouldn't have come.

And I shouldn't if I'm going to sob, she told herself. I will not cry.

The hymn came to an end. Kalifa's sons and brothers took up the coffin and carried it out of the chapel into the morning sun. From here it'd be taken to Atangi to be buried in the place of his ancestors.

Maddie wouldn't follow. Burial was the islanders' business. There'd be a wake later on but she wasn't up to a wake yet.

She turned away drearily, immeasurably sad for her friend. But life went on, she told herself. She needed to return to her daughter. She needed to get on with living. She turned towards the hospital—and Josh was right in front her.

Just…there.

'Hi,' he said, and she couldn't think of a single thing to say.

She was facing her husband. No. He was her ex-husband. He wasn't even the father of her child, she told herself desperately. He was someone who had nothing to do with her.

But that was a lie. He was someone who held her heart in his hands.

'I thought you were gone,' she said at last. It was a dumb thing to say but it was all she could think of. But she'd watched his plane take off. He should be in Cairns.

'I had a couple of things I forgot to say,' he said, and then he fell silent.

The hearse drove away, towards the harbour where a boat would carry Kalifa, in all honour, out to Atangi. The islanders followed.

The rest of the mourners drifted off. Maddie stood at the foot of the steps of the little island chapel and felt empty.

'Hey!' It was Caroline, flanked by Keanu and Hettie and Sam. Her people. 'Maddie needs to be back in bed,' Caroline said sternly. 'Thirty minutes tops, Dr Campbell, or we'll set Bugsy onto you.'

'See me terrified,' Josh called back, and Caroline chuckled and linked her arm in Keanu's and said something that made them all laugh—and then they were gone.

Her people.

Her husband?

'What...what did you need to say?' Maddie asked at last, because the silence was getting to her and, in truth, her legs ached and she wouldn't mind sitting down. And as if he guessed, Josh took her arm and led her to a wooden seat that looked out over the headland to the sea beyond.

It really was the most beautiful island. They were facing west, where the sun set. The island's sunsets were where the island got its name, for Wildfire was what they resembled.

Had Josh ever seen a Wildfire sunset?

She was babbling internally. She let herself be propelled to the seat and she tried to empty her mind.

Josh was still holding her arm. How could she empty her mind when all she could do was...feel?

'Two things,' he said into the stillness, and her heart seemed to stop.

'Two?'

'The first is that I'm sorry.' He wasn't looking at her. He was staring out at the distant sea, reflective, sad, almost as if looking back at those five past years. 'I'm sorry I left you. I'm sorry I was so weak.'

'You weren't weak.' She paused and stared down at her feet, thinking of all the times she'd tried to comfort him, all the times he'd held himself back. The bracing of his shoulders as she'd reached for him. The rigidity of his body, the sheer effort of holding emotion within. 'You were so strong I couldn't get near you.'

'But I wasn't strong enough. That was what I didn't see. That admitting weakness, admitting need, takes its own form of strength. That sharing is two-way. And that's the second thing I want to say to you, my Maddie. It's that I need you.'

I need you.

The words hung in the warm morning air.

Need.

He'd never said such a thing. Their relationship had been based on their love and her need. It hadn't been enough.

'How can you need me?' she whispered, hardly daring to breathe, and still he stared out to sea. His hands were clenched, as if things were breaking inside him, as if he was deliberately taking apart something he'd built over a lifetime.

'Because I'll shatter if you don't take me back,' he said, and then he shook his head. 'No. That's blackmail and there's no place for that here. I'll keep on going. I'll stay doing what I'm doing. But, Maddie, something inside me has changed. It's melted. When we were down the mine, when we'd delivered your daughter, when I thought we might die together, Maddie, I wanted to be held. I wanted to admit to you how scared I was. I was terrified for all of us. I was terrified of losing you, yet I couldn't admit it. And then...'

'Then?' How hard was it to whisper?

'Then we were safe and things were as they'd been before. I knew life could go on. I knew you didn't need me. But then I saw Nani come to visit you. She was bereft but she still came, to say to you that she knew you'd done your best, that there was no blame. And I thought, how strong was that? It's the kind of thing I might try—I have tried. When I'm hurt I try to make those around me feel better. It's what's been instilled in me since birth and I don't know any other way.'

'So what's different now?'

'I watched you,' he said simply. 'I watched you admit that you needed her. That you needed this island. Giving and taking. And all you've said to me... Everything over the years... It was like that moment coalesced it all. Maybe if I could have gone straight back to work, straight back into needed mode, I wouldn't have had time to sort it out, but Beth made me lie on the stretcher in the plane and I stared up at nothing and that moment kept coming back. And I thought...how selfish was I? To not let you care.'

'Josh...'

'I do need you, Maddie,' he told her, simply now and humbly. 'I've always needed you. I just didn't know how. Mikey's death shattered me and all I knew was to try and comfort you. I didn't see that sharing the hurt could have helped heal us both. And then, when Holly died so soon after, I was a mess and I kept thinking I couldn't lay that hurt on you. So stupidly, selfishly I stepped away. I told myself it was protecting you, but all the time it was about protecting my armour. I thought I'd shatter if I admitted need. But, Maddie, I do need. If anything happened to you now, I'd fall apart. If anything happened to Lea...'

And his voice broke.

Enough. She took him into her arms and pulled him to her. And he came. After all these years she felt him melt into her, merge, warmth against warmth. She felt him hold, not in passion but in need.

To take comfort.

To love.

How long they sat there she couldn't say. Up at the house Caroline would be caring for Lea, but she'd fed her just before the funeral. For now time didn't matter. It couldn't be allowed to matter.

All that mattered was that she was holding the man she loved.

'I wouldn't mind a kiss.'

She wasn't sure when she said it, or even why she said it, but suddenly it was needful. Comfort was all very well, she thought, but if she was getting her Josh back... Well, she wanted her Josh back. Bravado and all. Hero, except in the most dire of circumstances. Her knight in shining armour—but with the ability to take off his armour and leave it in the hall cupboard.

But then she was no longer thinking. There was no room for thinking because she was being soundly, ruthlessly kissed. She was in Josh's arms and there was nowhere else in the world she would have rather been.

She was with her Josh. He needed her.

She had her baby. She had her Josh.

She had her family.

Afterwards, when there was room for words again, when the world had somehow righted itself on this new and wonderful axis, she did check the hall cupboard. It took some doing but Josh had been gone for five long years and she wasn't about to let him back into her world on a promise. The sensible side of her—the part that had learned to distrust and could never completely be ignored—wanted to know just what terms that armour would be let out.

'So...' she managed, breathlessly because that kiss had taken energy and she didn't have much energy spare at the moment. 'So how could we work this? Because... Josh, you know that I love you but...'

'But my proposition about a house close to my work didn't make you happy?'

'You make me happy,' she said simply. 'But, Josh...'

'You love this island,' he said, cupping her face and kissing her again, lightly this time, tenderly, as if he had all the time in the world, and kissing her was almost as natural as breathing. 'I can see that. And you love this community and this community needs you. And you love your mum. Your mum needs you and you need your mum. And of course there's Lea, who we both love...'

'You don't...you don't mind that I used a sperm donor?'

'If I ever meet him I'll give him half my kingdom,' Josh said simply. 'He's given me a daughter—if you'll let me share.'

'Oh, Josh.' She could feel the tears. It was weakness, she thought desperately. She hated tears, but Josh smiled and kissed them away and she thought maybe she didn't hate them so much.

'Proposition,' he said simply. 'I've been talking to Keanu.'

'When?'

'Yesterday. When you were faffing about, learning how to feed your daughter. When he was faffing about, worrying about clots on my leg. He talked to me about these islands. He talked about how desperate the islanders are for a full medical service. Apparently the Lockhart money has run dry for the mine, but there's still Australian government funding for doctors—if you can get doctors to come here. They work on a doctors-per-head-of-population ratio, which means the islands are short by at least two, possibly three doctors. So I thought, if it's okay with you, I could come here. This is really tentative—I need to talk to Keanu and Sam—but it seems to me that a couple of doctors settled out on Atangi could work well. I could be part of the emergency on-call roster from there. It's only three minutes by chopper to pick me up. We could run a permanent clinic. We could build ourselves a great house overlooking the sea—'

'Josh…'

'We could be happy there,' he said, urgently now. 'I know we could. Sure, we'd be two doctors dependent on each other for backup, but…' He shrugged his shoulders and gave a rueful smile. 'I guess that's what you already know and I'm finding out. We could depend on each other. I'd need you, my Maddie, and you'd need me.'

'Josh.' Dammit, her eyes were brimming again. It sounded wonderful—it sounded brilliant—but there were still things…complications…

Love.

'Josh, I need to stay flying in and flying out.' It nearly killed her to say it but she had to. 'Or…or leave the islands and live in Cairns. It might need to be in your house near your work. Because Mum…'

'Your mum needs you.'

'I need my mum.' She said it simply. It was two-way, this loving business, and he had to see it. 'I can't walk away.'

'I would never ask you to.' Once more he kissed her. 'It's a whole, complex web. I need you, you need your mum,

I need you to be happy and you can't be happy without your mum. But there are needs and needs. There's another thought, as well. Your friend, Nani, loves Atangi and wants to live there, only of course she and Kalifa mortgaged their house to try and get her son out of debt. She loves you. This is early days, there's so much to sort out, but I thought, if we build big with a housekeeper's apartment, maybe we could bring your mother here. And Nani could be our housekeeper-carer. It'd mean your mother would be near Lea as she grows up. You'd have company if I'm called away. Maybe…maybe we could all be happy?'

And that pretty much took her breath away. She sat, astounded, as what he was proposing sank in.

A house on Atangi. No, a home. Her daughter, her mother, Bugsy, Nani…

Her husband.

Maybe even…

'Two or three?' Josh said, and grinned because he knew what she was thinking—he'd always known what she was thinking. 'We wouldn't want to be lonely. And maybe another pup to keep Bugsy company. After all, he saved your life—he deserves his own happy ending.'

'You'd do all that for me?' she whispered, and he cupped her face in his hands and his gaze met hers. He was loving her with his eyes.

'No,' he said softly. 'I'd do all that for me. I'd do it because I need it. I need you. I need family. Yes, I need to be needed, but I can be, and it will be two-way. I promise you, Maddie, love. If you'll marry me again I swear that I'll need you for as long as we both shall live.'

And what was a woman to say to that? There was only one answer and it was a soundless one.

She drew him to her and she kissed him, tenderly this time, lovingly, an affirmation of everything in her heart.

The armour was melting, she thought. Wherever he'd stowed it, she could feel it disappearing.

He had no need of armour.

Her heart was beating in sync with his. She loved and she loved and she loved.

Soon her daughter would need feeding. *Their* daughter.

They'd walk back to the house together, and they'd walk slowly because both of them hurt.

They'd hold each other up, she thought as he helped her to her feet.

They needed each other, and together it didn't hurt at all.

* * * * *

MILLS & BOON®
Hardback – March 2016

ROMANCE

The Italian's Ruthless Seduction	Miranda Lee
Awakened by Her Desert Captor	Abby Green
A Forbidden Temptation	Anne Mather
A Vow to Secure His Legacy	Annie West
Carrying the King's Pride	Jennifer Hayward
Bound to the Tuscan Billionaire	Susan Stephens
Required to Wear the Tycoon's Ring	Maggie Cox
The Secret That Shocked De Santis	Natalie Anderson
The Greek's Ready-Made Wife	Jennifer Faye
Crown Prince's Chosen Bride	Kandy Shepherd
Billionaire, Boss...Bridegroom?	Kate Hardy
Married for their Miracle Baby	Soraya Lane
The Socialite's Secret	Carol Marinelli
London's Most Eligible Doctor	Annie O'Neil
Saving Maddie's Baby	Marion Lennox
A Sheikh to Capture Her Heart	Meredith Webber
Breaking All Their Rules	Sue MacKay
One Life-Changing Night	Louisa Heaton
The CEO's Unexpected Child	Andrea Laurence
Snowbound with the Boss	Maureen Child

MILLS & BOON®
Large Print – March 2016

ROMANCE

A Christmas Vow of Seduction	Maisey Yates
Brazilian's Nine Months' Notice	Susan Stephens
The Sheikh's Christmas Conquest	Sharon Kendrick
Shackled to the Sheikh	Trish Morey
Unwrapping the Castelli Secret	Caitlin Crews
A Marriage Fit for a Sinner	Maya Blake
Larenzo's Christmas Baby	Kate Hewitt
His Lost-and-Found Bride	Scarlet Wilson
Housekeeper Under the Mistletoe	Cara Colter
Gift-Wrapped in Her Wedding Dress	Kandy Shepherd
The Prince's Christmas Vow	Jennifer Faye

HISTORICAL

His Housekeeper's Christmas Wish	Louise Allen
Temptation of a Governess	Sarah Mallory
The Demure Miss Manning	Amanda McCabe
Enticing Benedict Cole	Eliza Redgold
In the King's Service	Margaret Moore

MEDICAL

Falling at the Surgeon's Feet	Lucy Ryder
One Night in New York	Amy Ruttan
Daredevil, Doctor...Husband?	Alison Roberts
The Doctor She'd Never Forget	Annie Claydon
Reunited...in Paris!	Sue MacKay
French Fling to Forever	Karin Baine

MILLS & BOON®
Hardback – April 2016

ROMANCE

The Sicilian's Stolen Son	Lynne Graham
Seduced into Her Boss's Service	Cathy Williams
The Billionaire's Defiant Acquisition	Sharon Kendrick
One Night to Wedding Vows	Kim Lawrence
Engaged to Her Ravensdale Enemy	Melanie Milburne
A Diamond Deal with the Greek	Maya Blake
Inherited by Ferranti	Kate Hewitt
The Secret to Marrying Marchesi	Amanda Cinelli
The Billionaire's Baby Swap	Rebecca Winters
The Wedding Planner's Big Day	Cara Colter
Holiday with the Best Man	Kate Hardy
Tempted by Her Tycoon Boss	Jennie Adams
Seduced by the Heart Surgeon	Carol Marinelli
Falling for the Single Dad	Emily Forbes
The Fling That Changed Everything	Alison Roberts
A Child to Open Their Hearts	Marion Lennox
The Greek Doctor's Secret Son	Jennifer Taylor
Caught in a Storm of Passion	Lucy Ryder
Take Me, Cowboy	Maisey Yates
His Baby Agenda	Katherine Garbera

0316 GEN STD HB

MILLS & BOON®
Large Print – April 2016

ROMANCE

The Price of His Redemption	Carol Marinelli
Back in the Brazilian's Bed	Susan Stephens
The Innocent's Sinful Craving	Sara Craven
Brunetti's Secret Son	Maya Blake
Talos Claims His Virgin	Michelle Smart
Destined for the Desert King	Kate Walker
Ravensdale's Defiant Captive	Melanie Milburne
The Best Man & The Wedding Planner	Teresa Carpenter
Proposal at the Winter Ball	Jessica Gilmore
Bodyguard...to Bridegroom?	Nikki Logan
Christmas Kisses with Her Boss	Nina Milne

HISTORICAL

His Christmas Countess	Louise Allen
The Captain's Christmas Bride	Annie Burrows
Lord Lansbury's Christmas Wedding	Helen Dickson
Warrior of Fire	Michelle Willingham
Lady Rowena's Ruin	Carol Townend

MEDICAL

The Baby of Their Dreams	Carol Marinelli
Falling for Her Reluctant Sheikh	Amalie Berlin
Hot-Shot Doc, Secret Dad	Lynne Marshall
Father for Her Newborn Baby	Lynne Marshall
His Little Christmas Miracle	Emily Forbes
Safe in the Surgeon's Arms	Molly Evans

MILLS & BOON®

Why shop at millsandboon.co.uk?

Each year, thousands of romance readers find their perfect read at millsandboon.co.uk. That's because we're passionate about bringing you the very best romantic fiction. Here are some of the advantages of shopping at www.millsandboon.co.uk:

* **Get new books first**—you'll be able to buy your favourite books one month before they hit the shops

* **Get exclusive discounts**—you'll also be able to buy our specially created monthly collections, with up to 50% off the RRP

* **Find your favourite authors**—latest news, interviews and new releases for all your favourite authors and series on our website, plus ideas for what to try next

* **Join in**—once you've bought your favourite books, don't forget to register with us to rate, review and join in the discussions

Visit **www.millsandboon.co.uk**
for all this and more today!